BEASTLY BUSINESS

Also by THE BEASTLY BOYS

Werewolf versus Dragon

Sea Monsters and other Delicacies

Bang Goes a Troll

Battle of the Zombies

THE JUNGLE VAMPIRE

BY THE BEASTLY BOYS

ILLUSTRATED BY JONNY DUDDLE

SIMON AND SCHUSTER

SIMON AND SCHUSTER
First published in Great Britain in 2009
by Simon and Schuster UK Ltd
A CBS COMPANY
This paperback edition published in 2011.

Simon & Schuster UK Ltd
1st Floor, 222 Gray's Inn Road, London WC1X 8HB.

This book is a work of fiction. Names, characters, places and incidents are either
the product of the author's imagination or are used fictitiously. Any resemblance
to actual people living or dead, events or locales is entirely coincidental.

A CIP catalogue record for this book is available from the British Library.

ISBN: 978-0-85707-192-7

1 3 5 7 9 10 8 6 4 2

Printed and bound by CPI Group (UK) Ltd, Croydon, CR0 4YY

www.simonandschuster.co.uk

TONIGHT,

LOOK UP AT THE MOON.

LOOK AT IT CLOSELY.

STARE AT IT.

NOW ASK YOURSELF:

AM I FEELING BRAVE?

BEASTLY BUSINESS

CHAPTER ONE

Late one night, on the outskirts of a grimy town, a man in a long fur coat hurried through the rain. He held a black umbrella, hiding his face in shadow as he passed beneath the street lamps and turned down a quiet backstreet. He strode to the door of a warehouse, looked left then right, then knocked three times.

From inside came a voice: 'Who goes there?'

'It's me, you fool,' the man hissed. 'Open up.'

There came a scraping sound of a bolt being slid across. The door squeaked open and in the entrance to the warehouse stood a small man in a ragged suit. 'Sorry, Baron Marackai. You said not to let anyone in.'

'I meant strangers, Blud, you imbecile!'

Baron Marackai barged inside and whacked the small man with his umbrella. 'Well? Is it ready?' he asked.

'Not yet, Sir,' Blud replied.

The Baron looked to the end of the warehouse where a rickety flying machine was being assembled. It had two black wings and an open cockpit with a machine gun mounted to its front. Crawling over it were a dozen Helping Hands, small hand-shaped beasts, clutching spanners, tightening nuts and bolts.

'*Why* isn't it finished?' Baron Marackai yelled. 'It's supposed to be a *quick-assembly* flying machine!'

A big, bearded man was standing at the end of the warehouse holding a long whip. 'The little blighters won't do as they're told, Sir,' he said.

'Then whip them harder, Bone, you wimp!' The Baron marched over and snatched the big man's whip. He cracked it against the knuckles of a Helping Hand. 'Work faster!' he ordered it.

'I don't think they like being whipped, Sir,' Bone said.

'Good,' Baron Marackai replied. He cracked the whip again, even harder. The Helping Hand flinched, then it hurriedly began tightening a row of screws along the wing of the flying machine. Other Helping Hands scuttled to assist it. Two bolted a propeller to the front of the flying machine and more attached wheels to its base.

'That's more like it,' the Baron said. He paced around the machine, inspecting it closely. 'The perfect weapon,' he muttered.

The small man, Blud, scuttled over and tugged on the Baron's wet fur coat. 'Excuse me, Sir, but why do we need a flying machine?'

The Baron swivelled the gun on its front. 'Because we're going hunting.'

'Hunting for what, Sir?' Blud asked.

The Baron stroked the barrel of the gun. 'We're going hunting for a beast,' he said. 'A beast more terrifying than any you could possibly imagine.' He leant down to Blud, his

4

twisted face grinning. 'And when we find it, we're going to kill it.'

Blud smiled nervously. 'But what about you-know-who, Sir?' he asked.

'Those fools? Pa!' the Baron spat. 'They'll never catch us.' He raised his right hand. There was a small fleshy stump where his little finger was missing. 'Now repeat after me: death to the RSPCB!'

Blud and Bone raised their right hands and turned down their little fingers. 'Death to the RSPCC,' they mumbled.

'The RSPC*B*, you nincompoops!'

The Baron snatched a Helping Hand from the flying machine and slapped it across Blud's face. Then he poked Bone in the eye with its finger. 'Well, don't just stand there! Get ready!' he ordered. 'WE FLY TONIGHT!'

CHAPTER TWO

Two days later, at the Royal Society for the Prevention of Cruelty to Beasts, Ulf was in the big beast barn tending to a pegasaur. The winged horse had been brought into the rescue centre after its nest had become waterlogged in recent rains. It was suffering from a case of hoof-rot. Ulf had scrubbed its hooves with a wire brush and was filing them carefully with a metal rasp.

The RSPCB cared for all kinds of beasts, from sick sea monsters to trolls with toothache, from frostbitten dragons to fairies with broken wings. Ulf enjoyed helping to mend them.

He sprayed the pegasaur's hooves with anti-

6

fungal spray, then checked its hairy white **wings for** lice and ticks. 'You'll be as good as **new** soon,' he said to it. He gave it some hay to eat, then stepped out into the yard, closing the wooden doors behind him.

'Fur Face want some?' he heard. Ulf glanced up at Farraway Hall, a large country mansion – the headquarters of the RSPCB. On the rooftop, a gargoyle was picking earwax from its ear. 'Fur Face want some?' the gargoyle said again. It leered down and flicked the earwax at Ulf.

Ulf dodged. 'Missed me, Druce,' he said, laughing. Quickly, Ulf ran to the yard tap to wash his hands. He could hear the gargoyle gurgling. It was eating its breakfast, licking its ear with its yellow tongue. He could hear beasts in the beast park, roaring and squawking. The rains had stopped and they were enjoying the sunshine. Ulf smiled. It was a bright, cheery day.

To look at Ulf, washing his hands and drying them on his T-shirt, it would be easy to mistake him for a human boy. But if you looked closely, you'd notice the hair on his palms. For Ulf was a beast himself. Every month, on the night of the full moon, he'd transform from boy to wolf. Ulf was a werewolf.

He glanced across the yard to the feedstore, a tall wooden building with double doors. The doors were open, and inside he could see Orson the giant loading a huge rucksack with tins. Ulf went to see him. 'What are you doing, Orson?' he asked, peering in the doorway.

The giant looked over. 'Just getting something ready for Dr Fielding,' he replied.

Ulf glanced back towards Farraway Hall. Through a window on the ground floor, he could see Dr Fielding in her office. 'She's been in there all morning,' Ulf said. 'And last night. I saw her light on. What's she up to?'

'I'm afraid I'm not to say, Ulf,' the giant told him.

'Not to say *what*?'

Ulf saw the giant open the meats fridge and take out six packs of sausages.

'Sorry, Ulf, I can't chat now. There's lots to do before we go.'

'Go?' Ulf asked. 'Go where?'

The giant chuckled. 'Like I said, I'm not to tell. Top secret it is. Dr Fielding's orders.' He carried the rucksack to the back of the feedstore and began looking along the shelves, whistling to himself.

Ulf glanced back to Dr Fielding's office. The window was open. He crept across the yard, keeping low, and peered over the window ledge. A bright sparkle was hovering above Dr Fielding's desk. It was Tiana the fairy, Ulf's best friend. He listened, hearing Dr Fielding talking to her.

'You'll love it there, Tiana,' Dr Fielding said. 'There'll be all kinds of flowers with rare pollens to collect, so be sure to bring your satchel.'

'I'll fetch it right away,' Tiana replied. In a burst of sparkles the little fairy flew out through the window, zooming over Ulf's head.

'Psst,' he said to her.

Tiana stopped in mid-air. 'Ulf, are you snooping?' she whispered. The fairy swooped down and perched on his shoulder. She was dressed in camouflage, wearing a new dress made from blades of grass and creeper twine.

'You're all going somewhere, aren't you?' Ulf asked.

Tiana giggled. 'Whatever gave you that idea?'

Ulf eyed the fairy suspiciously, then peered back over the window ledge and saw Dr Fielding stand up and take an empty mug from her desk. She walked to the door and left her office. Quickly, he climbed in through the window to see what she'd been up to.

'Ulf, you shouldn't go in there,' Tiana called.

Ulf crept to Dr Fielding's desk. It was strewn with books, maps and RSPCB papers. A magazine was laid open at a page with a photograph of butterflies ringed in red pen. Ulf picked the magazine up. Beneath the photograph he read a caption:

Speckled Bluetails at Drake's Ridge, emailed from the Maripossa Mountains by butterfly photographer Hurricane Stoat

Ulf looked back at Tiana who was hovering

at the windowsill. 'Why's she reading about butterflies?' he asked.

Tiana twiddled a blade of grass on her dress. 'Maybe she likes them,' she said cagily.

Ulf heard footsteps coming back down the corridor. Hurriedly, he crawled under the desk to hide. He peeked out, seeing Dr Fielding's boots as she came back in. She walked over, and he heard her place her mug on the desk.

'Tiana, have you seen my copy of *Wildlife Weekly*?' Dr Fielding asked.

Ulf heard Tiana giggling on the windowsill. He had the magazine in his hand. A moment later, Dr Fielding's face appeared under the desk and he smiled, embarrassed.

'Cosy down there, are you, Ulf?' she asked.

'The game's up, werewolf,' Tiana said, laughing.

Ulf crawled out and handed Dr Fielding the magazine. 'I was only er… um…'

Dr Fielding frowned at him. 'Snooping, it's called, Ulf.'

'Sorry, Dr Fielding.'

11

Dr Fielding took a sip from her mug of coffee and smiled. 'Well, seeing as you're here, there's something I'd like to show you.' She picked up a dusty folder from her desk and handed it to him. 'This is one of Professor Farraway's old expedition files.'

Ulf held the folder excitedly. Professor Farraway had been the world's first cryptozoologist and the founder of the RSPCB. On the front of the folder Ulf saw EXPEDITION MANCHAY written in the Professor's handwriting. 'What's Manchay?' he asked.

'Manchay is a wild beast habitat, Ulf,' Dr Fielding told him. 'It's a remote jungle in South America.'

Ulf opened the folder. Inside were photographs of jungle beasts: winged beasts, armoured beasts, aquatic beasts and more.

'It's also one of the only places on earth where beasts and humans have lived together,' Dr Fielding added.

'Humans? Living with beasts?' Ulf said.

'Thousands of years ago, Manchay was home to a human tribe,' Dr Fielding explained. She picked out a photograph of gravestones overgrown with jungle vines and creepers. 'This is their burial ground, Ulf.'

In the photograph, among the graves, Ulf could see ghostly shadows with hollow eyes.

'Those are called encantos,' Dr Fielding said. 'They're the spirits of the ancient tribe. Professor Farraway photographed them on his expedition.'

Ulf looked closely at the photograph, imagining the spirits as a human tribe thousands of years ago living in the jungle.

'The Professor is the only person to have set foot in Manchay for centuries. He'd heard stories of spine-tingling screeches coming from the jungle at night. He had a theory that they were the cries of a very rare beast.'

'What beast?' Ulf asked.

'A jungle vampire,' Dr Fielding said.

'A *vampire*?'

Ulf had never seen a vampire before. He looked through the photographs searching for a picture of it. 'I can't see it here,' he said.

'That's because the Professor returned without finding it. I'd always assumed that maybe it didn't exist – until now.' Dr Fielding opened her copy of *Wildlife Weekly* and turned to the page showing the photograph of the butterflies ringed in red pen. 'Have a look at this, Ulf. This picture was taken by a photographer named Hurricane Stoat on a mountain range overlooking Manchay.'

'Butterflies?' Ulf asked.

'Look at the rock they're settled on.'

Ulf looked carefully. On the rock, between the butterflies, he could just make out faint carved lines.

'That's a tribal carving, Ulf.'

The lines formed an image of a winged beast with fangs.

'It's a vampire,' Dr Fielding said. 'The tribe must have known of the beast. I think it could still be out there.'

Ulf looked up from the photograph. 'After all this time?'

'Vampires can live indefinitely if there's blood for them to drink,' Dr Fielding told him. 'What do you say we go and look for it?'

'We?' Ulf asked.

'I've been observing you recently, Ulf, and I think you're ready to begin your training.'

'What training?'

'To become an official RSPCB agent. If that's what you'd like.'

'Yes, please!' Ulf said excitedly.

'Manchay will be the perfect place for you to learn about jungle beasts.'

Ulf could hardly believe what he was hearing. Dr Fielding never normally invited him on expeditions to the wild. He'd been just once, to the Jotunheim mountains of Norway, and only then because he'd stowed away.

'The search for the vampire should be quite an adventure, Ulf. Tiana will be coming.'

Ulf looked across at the little fairy perched on the windowsill.

'Surprise,' she giggled.

'I knew something was going on,' Ulf said.

'Orson's coming too,' Dr Fielding told him. Outside in the yard, Ulf could see Orson striding to the kit room. The giant was carrying his rucksack on his back. 'Why don't you go and help get the kit ready, Ulf.' Dr Fielding glanced at her wristwatch. 'We're due to leave in twenty minutes.'

CHAPTER THREE

'Ready for the jungle, Ulf?' Orson called. The giant was kneeling outside the kit room. He was too big to fit through the door and was reaching in with his long arm.

Ulf was running across the yard towards him. 'You knew all along, Orson,' he said.

The giant chuckled, pulling out a bundle of hammocks. 'You're going to love Manchay, Ulf. We'll be sleeping in the wild, under the stars.'

Ulf longed to see the wild. All his life he'd lived at the rescue centre, ever since he'd been brought there as a werecub.

'What do we need, Orson?' he asked, stepping inside the kit room and looking along the shelves of RSPCB equipment.

'Pass me the climbing ropes, please, Ulf,' the giant said.

Ulf passed Orson two long ropes from a hook on the wall, and the giant tied them to his rucksack. Ulf gathered mosquito nets, water bottles, torches, blankets, a two-way radio, and some pots and pans for cooking on a campfire. He couldn't wait to be in the jungle. He imagined the vampire soaring above the trees, screeching. 'Have you ever seen a vampire, Orson?' he asked.

'Not a jungle vampire,' the giant replied. 'I've seen a Redwing in India and a Half-blood in Transylvania. There used to be lots of vampires: Leatherbacks, Longhairs and even Pygmy vampires, but humans took a dislike to them. Killed most of them, they did.'

'*Killed* them?' Ulf asked. 'Why?'

Orson shrugged. 'Scared of them probably.' He was loading the kit into his rucksack. 'That's all in the past though, Ulf. Professor Farraway had a law passed that stopped it.

Vampires are a protected species nowadays.'

At that moment, Ulf heard a gurgled cry: 'Vammmpuuurgh!'

He looked over and saw Druce the gargoyle on the roof of the hatching bay, flapping his stubby little wings. The gargoyle jumped on to the roof of the kit room and leered down at Ulf, drooling two long strands of spit like vampire fangs.

'That's pretty, Druce,' Ulf said, laughing.

Orson chuckled. 'Playing vampire, are you?'

'Vampurgh scary,' the gargoyle gurgled. He looked over slyly as a sparkle came flying across the yard towards them. It was Tiana.

'Orson, Dr Fielding says not to forget to pack her medical gear,' the little fairy said.

The gargoyle flicked out his long yellow tongue, soaking the fairy in spit.

'Eeyugh!' Tiana shrieked, shaking her wings. 'That's horrible, Druce.' She blasted sparkles at the gargoyle's nose, then zoomed off over the big beast barn. 'Don't go without me,' she called. 'I've just got to fetch my satchel.'

Ulf stuck out his tongue at Druce and the gargoyle grinned.

'Right,' Orson said, lifting his rucksack on to his back. 'Thanks for your help, Ulf. I'll fetch Dr Fielding's medical gear, then we'll be ready to leave.' The giant strode towards the side door of Farraway Hall.

'I'll be with you in a minute,' Ulf called to him, then he raced out of the yard to a small stone hut at the side of the paddock. It had bars on the door and the windows. This was Ulf's den. There was something he wanted to check. Ulf went inside and knelt in the straw on the floor, pulling out a loose brick from the back wall. Behind it, from his secret hiding place, he took out *The Book of Beasts*, an old notebook that had belonged to Professor Farraway. It contained secrets on every beast imaginable. Ulf looked through the pages, flicking past a sketch of a mermaid's skeleton, tips on growing ghost plants, and jottings on the calls and whistles of mimis. He found a section headed: VAMPIRES

Vampires are nocturnal beasts that hunt the blood of live prey. Commonly misunderstood to be evil, they are driven by a simple dietary need, since they lack the ability to produce blood of their own. While a vampire's victim will normally die from an attack, vampires do not intend to kill but merely to feed. Indeed, I have seen rare instances of donor beasts offering their blood to a vampire without struggle and their lives being spared.

'Lights out. Go to sleep. What's that nibbling on your feet? Vampuuuurgh!'

Ulf heard a gurgling sound coming from above. 'Is that you, Druce?' he called, slipping *The Book of Beasts* into its hiding place. Ulf stepped outside and saw the gargoyle sitting on the roof of his den.

'Fur Face going now?' Druce asked, pointing to the sky. In the distance, Ulf noticed a plane flying towards the beast park.

He turned and saw Orson striding down the

side of the paddock with the rucksack on his back. 'Are we going by plane, Orson?' he asked.

'It's a C130 Hercules,' Orson said. 'An old tank transporter, courtesy of the Royal Air Force.'

Ulf heard the plane's engine roar as it soared over the seawater lagoon and the Great Grazing Grounds. It banked in a wide arc over the Dark Forest. It was coming into land in the paddock. Wheels lowered from its undercarriage, and the plane touched down bumping along the grass.

Ulf had never been in a plane before. He watched excitedly as it came to a halt and a large ramp lowered at its back, its cargo hold opening.

'Big enough to carry a giant,' Orson said.

Ulf could hear winged beasts squawking in the aviary. The plane had disturbed them. He looked up at Orson, concerned. 'Who's going to look after the beasts while we're away?' he asked.

Druce leapt from the roof of Ulf's den. 'Me will!' the gargoyle said. 'Drucey keep watch.' With a happy gurgling sound, the gargoyle scampered back to Farraway Hall and began climbing up to the roof.

'Don't worry, Ulf. I've made arrangements,' Orson whispered. The giant pointed to the track leading to the yard. A group of Helping Hands were dragging sacks of feed out to the beast park. A crate full of them had come into the rescue centre the day before, having been found on a rubbish dump. 'A bar of soap and a bucket of water and they soon scrubbed up, eager to help,' Orson said. 'Druce won't have to do a thing.'

Ulf smiled, seeing Druce hanging from a drainpipe at the top of the house, licking bricks.

Dr Fielding came hurrying from the yard, dressed in jungle camouflage. 'Right then, let's go,' she called, heading towards the plane.

Ulf was about to follow when he noticed a curtain moving in a window on the middle floor of Farraway Hall. It was the window of the old library. The curtain was nudging open and Ulf could see the tiny light of a candle flickering behind the glass. *Professor Farraway!* he thought.

'Come on, Ulf!' Orson called.

Ulf turned and saw the giant striding to the plane following Dr Fielding. A sparkle zoomed out of the Dark Forest as Tiana flew to join them. 'I'll just be a minute!' Ulf called. He sprinted back to the house and ran in through the side door then up the back stairs. He dashed along the Gallery of Science and through the Room of Curiosities to the door of the old library. The door creaked open and Ulf heard moaning and groaning inside. He stepped into the gloom and the candle came drifting towards him. 'Professor?' he asked. 'What's up?'

Ulf knew something that even Dr Fielding didn't. Professor Farraway was now a ghost and haunted the library at Farraway Hall.

The flickering candle drifted down to a dusty table. By the light of its flame, an invisible finger began writing in the dust:

BEWARE THE SIXTH SWORD

Ulf stared at the words. 'Professor, what do you mean?'

'Ulf! Everyone's waiting,' he heard. He glanced round and saw Tiana flying in, sparkling.

'Tiana, look at this,' he said.

The fairy hovered by his shoulder staring at

the words. 'Beware the sixth sword?' she read. 'What's that all about?'

'The Professor wrote it,' Ulf told her.

Tiana frowned. 'Come on, we haven't got time for spooky messages,' she said.

Ulf glanced at the candle. 'Sorry, Professor, but I have to go,' he told the ghost.

'I'll race you,' Tiana called. She flew out of the library and Ulf ran after her.

At the doorway, he glanced back over his shoulder. 'Professor, I'm sorry. I've got a plane to catch,' he said. 'I'm off on expedition – to look for the jungle vampire.' Ulf watched as the candle flame sputtered and went out. He sprinted downstairs, through the house and out the side door. In the paddock, the plane's propellers were spinning. It was ready for take-off.

'Quickly, Ulf, we're waiting,' Dr Fielding called from the plane.

Ulf and Tiana hurried across the paddock and climbed up into the cockpit beside her.

'Ulf, Tiana, I'd like you to meet our pilot,' Dr Fielding said. 'Squadron Leader T-Bone Steel of the Royal Air Force. He's an old friend of mine.'

At the plane's controls sat a square-jawed man in a blue uniform. He was flicking switches and setting dials. 'Prepare for take off,' he said.

Ulf buckled himself in as the plane began moving. He glanced out of the window at Farraway Hall, thinking about Professor Farraway's message: *beware the sixth sword*. Why did the Professor write it?

The engine roared as the plane accelerated, thundering across the paddock. Ulf could feel his seat shaking. He held his breath as they lifted off the ground. The plane soared over the biodomes, then banked above Troll Crag and headed out over the sea.

'Destination: the Maripossa Mountains,' the pilot announced. 'Estimated time of arrival: eleven o'clock tomorrow morning.'

Ulf glanced down. Farraway Hall was already just a dot far below. Then everything went white as the plane flew up into the clouds. He smiled. **He was off to search for the jungle vampire!**

CHAPTER FOUR

Thousands of miles away in South America, Baron Marackai's rickety flying machine hurtled towards a rocky field. It landed with a thump, skidding and swerving between boulders, its metal frame shaking and its canvas wings bouncing. It juddered to a halt.

'Blud, you fool, you nearly killed us!' Baron Marackai yelled from the back of the cockpit.

Blud turned off the engine. 'Sorry, Sir, I've never flown a plane before.' He was in the front of the flying machine, gripping the control stick. Bone was squeezed in beside him, picking squashed flies from his face.

The Baron climbed out and dusted down his

long fur coat. 'Get the rucksacks,' he ordered.

'I thought we were going to the jungle, Sir,' Blud said. He was looking across the rocky field to more fields beyond it.

'We are, you idiot. The jungle's that way.' Baron Marackai pointed to a range of mountains in the distance. 'We'll continue our journey on foot. I don't want anyone seeing us arrive.' From inside his fur coat, the Baron pulled out a telescope and held it to his eye, scanning the mountains.

Blud and Bone climbed out and took three rucksacks from the back of the cockpit. One was huge.

'That big one's yours, Bone,' the Baron told him.

Bone opened it. 'But it's empty, Sir,' he said.

The Baron took a spanner and screwdriver from his coat pocket and threw them at Bone. 'Dismantle the flying machine and pack it away. You're carrying it.'

Bone looked at the huge contraption. 'But, Sir, we've only just assembl—'

'Stop complaining, you oaf. We'll need it later.' The Baron peered back through his telescope at the mountains and muttered under his breath: 'I'm coming to get you.'

Blud skittered to the Baron's side. 'Excuse me, Sir, but is it a giant monkey we're after?'

'No it's *not* a giant monkey, you fool,' the Baron spat.

'Then what is it?'

The Baron grinned. 'If I told you, you'd curdle with fright. Now stop bothering me and help dismantle that machine.'

While Blud and Bone worked, removing wheels and wings, the Baron sat on the grass and unzipped his rucksack. He took out a magazine and lay back, resting his feet on a boulder. 'Nice here, isn't it?' he said. 'The perfect place for a spot of light reading.' He opened the magazine and turned to a page with a photograph of butterflies settled on a rock. 'MY DESTINY,' he said.

BEASTLY BUSINESS

CHAPTER FIVE

The C130 Hercules flew through the night, all the way over the ocean. As the sun started to rise, Ulf looked down and saw they were now passing above hills and fields. The whole landscape was bathed in a pink light.

'It looks pretty from up high, doesn't it?' Tiana said. She was perched on the control panel in front of Squadron Leader Steel.

Dr Fielding leant across Ulf and pointed out of the window to a range of mountains on the horizon. 'Those are the Maripossa Mountains, Ulf. The jungle of Manchay is just beyond them.' Ulf saw that two of the mountains rose higher than the rest. 'The tall ones are known as the horns of Manchay. The flat ridge between them is Drake's Ridge where that photograph was taken.'

'We'll be reaching the drop site in thirty minutes,' the pilot said.

'Drop site?' Ulf asked.

Dr Fielding reached under Ulf's seat and pulled out a parachute packed in a bundle. 'You'll need this,' she said, handing it to him. 'We're going to parachute down on to Drake's Ridge. That's where our expedition begins.'

Ulf slipped the parachute on to his back.

'I'll start circling when we're there,' the pilot said.

'Thank you,' Dr Fielding replied. She got up from her seat and opened a hatch at the back of the cockpit. She stepped through it into the large cargo hold at the rear of the plane. Ulf and Tiana followed.

Orson was in the cargo hold, sitting hunched up, his head touching the ceiling. 'Are we ready to go, Dr Fielding?' he asked.

There was a loud roaring sound as the back

of the cargo hold opened and a strong wind blew inside. Ulf could see the sky.

'I'll go first,' Dr Fielding said, stepping to the open end of the plane.

'Dr Fielding, I've never done a parachute jump before,' Ulf called.

Dr Fielding smiled. 'There's nothing to it, Ulf. Just lean out and let yourself fall.' The wind was blowing her hair in all directions. 'Pull the rip-cord to release your parachute and use the shoulder straps to steer. When you land, bend your knees. Okay?'

Ulf gave a thumbs-up.

'You'll enjoy it,' Dr Fielding said. Then she leapt from the plane.

Ulf felt Orson's finger tap on his shoulder.

'You're next, Ulf,' the giant said.

Ulf stepped to the open end of the plane. He looked down, feeling the warm wind on his face. He could see a white speck far below. It was Dr Fielding's open parachute. She was above the horns of Manchay, descending to Drake's Ridge.

Tiana whizzed past his ear. 'Last one down's a loser,' she called, flying into the sky.

Ulf's heart was racing. His knees felt weak.

'Go for it, Ulf,' Orson said.

Ulf took a deep breath and jumped from the plane. He felt the wind rush past him and he somersaulted, tumbling and turning, falling through the air. He dropped like a stone. Then he pulled the rip-cord and his parachute opened, pulling him upright with a jolt. He dangled beneath it, drifting downwards.

Tiana zoomed around him, sparkling. 'Fun, isn't it, Ulf?' she said.

Ulf started to relax. As he glided downwards, he looked out over the mountains. The vast jungle of Manchay stretched into the distance. It looked bigger than he'd imagined. The jungle trees grew like a green blanket over the hills and valleys. He could see rivers, waterfalls and canyons.

Ulf tugged on the straps of his parachute, steering himself in the breeze. He was coming down between the horns of Manchay, descending towards a long green ridge. Butterflies were fluttering in the air around him. He could see Dr Fielding on the ground below. She'd landed and was gathering her parachute.

'Remember to bend your knees,' Tiana said.

Ulf pulled hard on both straps then bent his knees as his feet hit the ground. He skidded along the ridge, being dragged by the wind.

Dr Fielding caught him and steadied him. 'Well done, Ulf,' she said, gathering his parachute as it blew in the breeze.

'That was fantastic,' he told her, slipping it off his back. He was smiling.

'Welcome to the Maripossa Mountains.'

Ulf looked around. Either side of him were the high peaks of the horns of Manchay. Drake's Ridge was strewn with rocks and flowers. Butterflies were flitting among them.

'Mind out!' he heard from above. He looked up and saw Orson's big boots plumetting towards him. The giant was wearing four parachutes and carrying his huge rucksack in his arms. There was an almighty thud as he landed just metres away.

'That was close,' Orson said, smiling at Ulf. He placed his rucksack down then gathered his parachutes, pulling them in with his big hands.

Dr Fielding unzipped the rucksack's side pocket and took out the two-way radio. She turned it on and twiddled a dial. 'All down and safe,' she said into the mouthpiece.

'Good luck, Dr Fielding,' a crackly voice replied.

'Thank you, T-Bone.'

Ulf glanced up, seeing the plane fly off.

'Orson, would you prepare the climbing rope, please?' Dr Fielding asked. She hung a pair of binoculars around her neck, then took a piece of paper from her pocket. It was the page torn from *Wildlife Weekly* showing the photograph of the butterflies on the rock carving. She headed off along the ridge, looking at the ground.

'It's great here, isn't it, Ulf?' Tiana said, darting among a group of red and yellow butterflies.

Ulf looked out from the ridge over the jungle. 'Manchay's huge,' he said to her. 'How are we ever going to find a vampire down there?'

'Ulf, come and see this,' Dr Fielding called.

Ulf looked over. Dr Fielding was crouched beside a large flat rock overgrown with creepers. He ran to her. 'Recognise this?' she said, pulling the creepers aside.

On the rock, Ulf saw the carving of the winged beast with fangs. 'The vampire,' he said.

The rock carving looked much bigger in real life than it had in the photograph. Below it, Ulf saw another carving of a webbed foot with three toes. 'Dr Fielding, what's this other carving?' he asked, pointing to it.

'I'm not sure,' Dr Fielding replied. She pulled all the creepers from the rock, and Ulf saw more carvings. There was one of a long coiling snake, one of an eye and another of a mouth surrounded by leaves.

'How extraordinary,' Dr Fielding said.

'Are these *all* tribal carvings?' Ulf asked.

'They look like they are, Ulf.'

Tiana flew to the rock, darting from one carving to the next. 'I didn't think there'd be lots of them,' she said. Half way along the carving of the snake, she stopped. 'Look, it's got something in its belly.' There was a bulge in the snake's belly, and inside it was what looked like a carving of a pear. 'That's odd,' the little fairy said. 'Snakes don't eat pears.'

They were all looking at the carvings wonderingly, when Ulf heard a voice behind him. 'Nobody move.' He turned and saw a man in white shorts and a white jacket stepping along the ridge. The man had a white floppy hat and a big droopy moustache. Around his neck hung a camera, and in his hand was a butterfly net. 'Stay exactly where you are,' he told them.

Ulf looked at Dr Fielding. 'Who is—'

'Shh, you'll scare it away,' the man said. He crept to the rock with his net held in the air. In one clean swipe, he brought it down on top of Tiana. 'Got it,' he said, triumphantly.

'Hey, let me out!' Tiana called, struggling in the butterfly net.

The man gently picked Tiana out and held her up to take her photograph. 'My my, this is an unusual butterfly,' he said, looking at her through his camera lens.

'Let her go,' Ulf said. 'She's not a butterfly!'

'Tiana's a fairy,' Dr Fielding told the man.

'A fairy?' The man let go of Tiana and she flew into the air, crossly. He stared open-mouthed seeing her sparkling. Then he looked back at Ulf. 'Sorry, who did you say you were?'

'He didn't,' Tiana said, glaring at the man.

'We're from the RSPCB,' Ulf said.

'The Royal Society for the Prevention of Cruelty to Beasts,' Dr Fielding explained. 'My name's Dr Helen Fielding.' She smiled and held out her hand for the man to shake. 'And you must be Hurricane Stoat the butterfly photographer, I presume.'

The man shook her hand, gingerly. 'That's me. Do you know my work?'

Ulf glanced around the ridge wondering where the man had come from. 'What are you doing here?' he asked.

41

'I'm documenting the butterflies. I've been here six weeks now. In fact I was just photographing a rare Spotted-Tail on the mountainside over there when I heard voices. Here for a bit of butterfly spotting too are you?'

'We've come because of a photograph of yours in *Wildlife Weekly*,' Dr Fielding said.

'Ah, the Bluetails, I expect. Very rare butterflies those. I sent that photograph for publication the very moment I took it.'

'Mr Stoat, have you by chance heard a loud screeching sound at night?' Dr Fielding asked.

Hurricane Stoat looked at her, puzzled. 'A screeching sound?'

'A spine-tingling screeching sound,' Ulf said.

'Spine-tingling?' The photographer thought for a second. 'I've heard a few squawks.'

'Nothing else?' Dr Fielding asked.

'Maybe a hoot or two.'

'Hmm,' Dr Fielding said. 'No loud screeches?'

Hurricane Stoat was looking curiously at Ulf's hairy feet. 'Why aren't you wearing shoes?' he asked.

'I'm Ulf,' Ulf said. 'I'm a werewolf.'

Hurricane Stoat took a step back.

'It's okay, Mr Stoat, he won't bite,' Dr Fielding said. She glanced along the ridge. 'Orson, is the rope ready?' she called.

Orson had pegged the end of a climbing rope into the ground. It was pulled tight over the edge of the ridge and the giant was testing it. His head poked up. 'Ready when you are,' he called.

'Golly, he's a big fellow,' Hurricane Stoat said.

'Orson's a giant,' Ulf explained.

'Excuse me a second, please,' Dr Fielding said. She walked towards Orson. 'Orson, I think we'll explore the eastern sector first. After that we'll trek westwards.' Ulf saw Dr Fielding lift her binoculars and look out over Manchay. 'There's a gorge to the east. That's the type of place we may find its lair.' She took out a compass and notepad and began plotting the route.

Hurricane Stoat leant down to Ulf. 'Are you looking for something?' he whispered.

'We're searching for a vampire,' Ulf said.

Hurricane Stoat gulped. 'A vampire?'

'A jungle vampire.'

The photographer glanced around nervously. 'You mean there's a v-v-vampire round here?' He was clutching his butterfly net tightly. 'I'm camping on these mountains. What if it comes for me?'

Tiana circled around his head. 'I shouldn't worry, Mr Stoat. It probably won't like the taste of you,' she said, then she giggled and flew off to see Orson.

Ulf glanced out over Manchay, imagining the vampire down there somewhere in the jungle, hidden in its lair. He scanned the trees, his eyes following a winding river that coiled northwards through the landscape like a snake. The river had a bulge in its middle.

Snake! he thought. Ulf looked again at the carvings on the rock. He saw the bulging belly on the carving of the snake, and its long winding body. 'Dr Fielding, I think we should head north,' he called.

Dr Fielding looked over. 'North? Why, Ulf?'

Ulf pointed north over Manchay. 'Look at the shape of the river,' he told her.

Dr Fielding peered through her binoculars.

'It's got a wide section in its middle,' Ulf said.

'What about it?' Dr Fielding asked.

'Now look at this snake carving.'

Dr Fielding came over to see.

'They're the same shape,' Ulf said.

'How peculiar,' Dr Fielding muttered.

'What if it's a map?' Ulf asked. 'A tribal map.'

'It could be. Yes, it's certainly possible.'

Hurricane Stoat looked at the carvings on the rock. 'A map to where?' he asked.

Ulf felt his heart beating faster as his eyes weaved along the coils of the snake following it upwards to the carving of the vampire. 'To the vampire's lair,' he said.

'Orson, change of plan,' Dr Fielding called. 'We'll start by trekking to the river, then continue northwards from there.' She took a pencil from her pocket, and made a sketch of the carvings in her notepad. 'Good work, Ulf,' she said. Then she turned to Hurricane Stoat.

'Mr Stoat, it was nice to meet you, but we have to go now.' She held out her hand for him to shake. 'Good luck with your butterfly spotting.'

Hurricane Stoat gripped her hand tightly. 'Are you just going to leave me here?' he asked, his voice trembling.

'We came to explore Manchay,' Dr Fielding explained.

'But this werewolf tells me that there's a jungle vampire on the loose. I'm not being picked up for another ten days.'

Dr Fielding let go of his hand. 'Sorry, Mr Stoat. We have to go.'

'May I come with you?' the photographer asked.

'This is RSPCB business, Mr Stoat.'

'**But what if the vampire comes for me? What if I get eaten?**' The photographer dropped to his knees. 'Please,' he pleaded.

Orson stepped over. 'Are you all right, Mister?'

'Please let me come!' Hurricane Stoat begged him. 'I'd feel much safer with you to protect me.'

Orson lifted Mr Stoat to his feet. 'There's no need to get all worked up.'

'Very well, then, Mr Stoat,' Dr Fielding said. 'But you must stick close. There are beasts down in the jungle and it could be dangerous.'

'Oh, thank you. Thank you,' Hurricane Stoat replied. He held up his camera. 'I'll be the official RSPCB photographer. Say cheese.' He clicked a button and the camera flashed.

Ulf blinked from the bright light and rubbed his eyes as he followed Dr Fielding to the rope. 'Ulf, you can go first,' she said.

Eagerly, Ulf took hold of the climbing rope and lowered himself over the edge of the ridge. He began climbing down, hand over hand, descending into Manchay. From the trees below, he could hear muffled squawks, hoots and bellows. *Jungle beasts*, he thought excitedly.

CHAPTER SIX

Ulf climbed down the rope, descending through the treetops. He slid between branches and leaves, then dropped to the jungle floor. He looked around in awe. He'd never seen a place so green. The trees towered overhead, their branches spread in an emerald canopy. It was like being under a huge green umbrella. Shafts of afternoon light were leaking between the leaves and he saw pink and blue flashes as giant dragonflies swirled among them. High up, a rainbow parrot took off from its nest, trailing a kaleidoscope of colours, and a troop of sucker monkeys swung on their tentacles through the branches. He saw tall splaying ferns, waxy broad-leafed plants and bushes with big juicy berries.

Tiana zoomed down, sparkling among the flowers. 'This place is amazing,' she said. There were flowers of every colour with petals like trumpets, starbursts and bells.

One after the other, Orson, Dr Fielding and Hurricane Stoat climbed down from the rope into the jungle.

'Follow me,' the giant said, striding off through the trees. As he passed Ulf, he whispered to him: 'Make sure Mr Stoat's okay, will you?'

Ulf looked back at Hurricane Stoat. He was clutching his butterfly net, jabbing it at a plant, trying to shoo a huge spider from a leaf. The spider was growling at him.

'This way, Mr Stoat,' Ulf called. He followed Orson through a thicket of horse-tail ferns, his bare arms brushing against the plants. He could hear rattler roots moving across the jungle floor. He trod carefully, his bare feet scrunching on leaves.

'Keep an eye out for signs of the vampire,' Orson said.

Ulf checked tree trunks for claw marks and sniffed the air for the scent of blood.

'Ouch,' he heard. He looked back and saw Hurricane Stoat caught on the thorns of a porcupine bush. The photographer was trying to unhook his camera strap.

Tiana flew to Ulf's side, giggling. 'He's hopeless,' she said.

'Would you like some help, Mr Stoat?' Ulf called.

'No, no, I'm perfectly fine.'

Dr Fielding went to free the photographer anyway.

'Mind your head here, Ulf,' Orson called.

Ulf ducked under the arching roots of a jailer tree. The air felt hot and humid, and he could feel sweat trickling down his back as he trekked down to a stinky black swamp. It was bubbling with mudhoppers, spiky frog-like beasts, that were springing from the water, snatching flies from the air.

'Mind out of the way!' he heard. Ulf turned and saw Hurricane Stoat racing towards him being chased by a flying ant. Tiana giggled as the photographer ran into the swamp. 'Urgh!' he said, standing knee-deep in the water.

'Flying ants are nothing to be afraid of,' Ulf told him.

'That was a big one,' Hurricane Stoat said. He was glancing around nervously, but the jungle insect had gone.

'Stick with me,' Ulf told him. He helped Hurricane Stoat out, then clambered up a mound of slippery slimegrass to a clearing where small sun lizards were basking on the ground. A hammer-headed eagle swooped down and grabbed a lizard in its claws.

'Golly,' Hurricane Stoat said, clicking his camera to take a photograph.

Ulf led him carefully round the edge of the clearing, following Orson. The giant was striding through a grove of hive trees. Ulf could hear swarms of bees buzzing inside the trees' hollow branches. Golden juice was dripping from their leaves. Ulf tilted his head back as he walked. He opened his mouth, drinking the juice like rain.

'Be careful, that might be poisonous,' Hurricane Stoat said to him.

Ulf licked his lips and smiled. It was sticky, sweet, jungle honey.

Tiana was flying ahead through a bamboozle thicket, collecting the pollen from flowers. 'Look at this, Ulf,' she called. He hurried after her and saw a long hairy tail dangling down through the canopy.

'Snake!' Hurricane Stoat cried, seeing it.

Ulf laughed. 'It won't bite you, Mr Stoat.'

It was the tail of a giant sloth.

Tiana was giggling. 'I don't think Mr Stoat knows much about beasts,' she whispered.

'Mind how you go here,' Orson called, as they pushed out from the thicket.

Ulf saw bones scattered on the ground among trees and ferns. The giant was kneeling down inspecting them.

'What's happened here?' Ulf asked.

'They're dead monkeys and birds,' Orson said. 'Something's been feeding.'

'Feeding?' Hurricane Stoat asked nervously.

Dr Fielding stepped out behind him. She pointed up into the trees. 'Snapweeds by the looks of it – flesheating plants.'

Ulf looked up. In the branches he could see huge red pods the size of barrels. They were hanging from thick green creepers that coiled around the tree trunks.

Orson led the way. 'Go nice and easy,' he called. 'And don't brush against their stems. That's how they sense you.'

'Come on, everyone, it's simple,' Tiana said, darting after him. She flew high, weaving between the red pods.

Ulf glanced back at Dr Fielding. She was making notes in her notepad. 'You go on, Ulf,' she told him. 'I'll be right behind you.'

Ulf stepped forward, feeling bones crunch beneath his bare feet. Hurricane Stoat crept alongside, clicking his camera. Overhead, Ulf heard a red pod start to rumble.

'Why's it making that noise?' Hurricane Stoat whispered.

'It's probably hungry,' Ulf told him.

Hurricane Stoat grasped Ulf's arm. 'Hungry?'

A trail of juice dripped down from the big red pod and splashed on to Hurricane Stoat's hat. It was sticky and green. 'Urgh!' he said, wiping it off. 'What *is* this stuff?'

'It looks like plant saliva,' Ulf said.

Above them, the pod was opening like a large gummy mouth. It growled, then a fat green tongue poked out.

Hurricane Stoat cowered, quivering with fright. 'It's going to eat us,' he shrieked. He started running.

'Mr Stoat, be careful!'

Hurricane Stoat stumbled on the bones and knocked against the stem of a snapweed. Above him, another large red pod opened.

'Mind out, Mr Stoat!' Ulf called. The red pod lunged down and Ulf dived, pushing the photographer out of the way. The pod snapped shut around Ulf's legs and lifted him high into the air. It swung him upwards. 'Help!' he called. He was trapped in the flesheater's jaws.

'Ulf!' Dr Fielding cried.

Ulf was being dragged up through the branches. He was trying to prise the pod open, but it wouldn't let go of him. He could feel its teeth gripping him and its tongue licking. Saliva was running over his legs.

From down below came a white flash as Hurricane Stoat took a photograph. 'That's what I call an action shot!' he said.

Orson stepped over. 'Mind out the way, Mr Stoat. We'll have you down in just a second, Ulf.'

Ulf felt the snapweed's long tongue wrap around his waist. It was slurping and slobbering, pulling him further inside the large red pod.

Orson threw his rucksack down and rummaged inside it. 'Catch this, Ulf,' the giant said, throwing him a small white pot. 'Shake it in its mouth.'

Ulf caught the pot and, as the pod licked and nibbled him, he shook it. A fine black powder sprinkled out over the snapweed's tongue. All at once, Ulf heard a loud sharp growl like a sneeze, and the pod sprang open, spitting him out. He shot through the air and landed with a bump in a clump of ferns.

Dr Fielding ran over to him. 'Are you okay, Ulf?'

He sat up, wiping green goo from his trousers. 'I think so,' he said. He saw the red pod recoiling high into the branches, spitting and spluttering.

'Well done, Ulf,' Orson said, stepping over. The giant reached down and took the white pot from Ulf's hand. 'Good stuff, isn't it?'

'What is it, Orson?' Ulf asked.

'Pepper,' the giant chuckled. 'Flesheaters hate it.'

Ulf smiled.

'Up you get, Ulf,' Dr Fielding said. 'Let's get out of here before we get into any more trouble.'

Orson slung his rucksack over his shoulder and Hurricane Stoat dashed through the trees beside him. 'Bagsy I walk with the giant,' the photographer said.

Tiana perched on Ulf's shoulder and whispered in his ear. 'That silly Mr Stoat nearly got you eaten.'

As Ulf pushed himself up to leave, he felt something crack under his hand. He looked down. Among the ferns he saw two bony feet. He parted the leaves and saw two bony legs, then a ribcage, two arms and a skull. **It was a human skeleton.**

Tiana saw it and gasped. 'It's a person!' she said.

'Dr Fielding,' Ulf called.

Dr Fielding and Orson turned back.

'What's the matter, Ulf?' Dr Fielding asked. She saw the skeleton. 'Oh my word,' she said.

'He must have been an explorer,' Tiana said, hovering over the skeleton.

Ulf glanced to Dr Fielding. 'I thought only Professor Farraway had explored Manchay.'

'So did I, Ulf,' Dr Fielding replied.

'Then who's this?' Ulf asked. Beside the skeleton he noticed something glint. He brushed aside the leaves. The skeleton's hand was touching the handle of a shiny silver sword. Engraved along the sword's blade was a word: PILKINGTON.

'Don't touch that, Ulf,' Orson said, leaning

down. 'That thing could give you a nasty cut.' Orson plucked the sword from the skeleton's bony fingers.

'Why's he got a sword?' Tiana asked.

Ulf noticed Hurricane Stoat peering over his shoulder. 'I should think that's obvious,' the photographer said. 'To fend off these beastly plants.'

Orson placed the sword under his boot and bent back its handle, snapping it in two. 'Nasty things, swords,' he said, and he threw the broken pieces into the bushes. 'Come on, everyone. We should keep going.'

Ulf was staring at the skeleton. He was thinking back to the library at Farraway Hall, and the warning that the Professor's ghost had written in the dust: *beware the sixth sword*.

CHAPTER SEVEN

It was late afternoon by the time the RSPCB trekked clear of the snapweeds. Ulf and Tiana were trailing behind, talking.

'But you saw what the Professor wrote,' Ulf whispered. '*Beware the sixth sword.*'

'Ulf, it's just a coincidence,' Tiana replied. 'Anyway, that sword's broken now.' She was weaving among tall ferns and enormous buttress trees with trunks over ten metres wide. 'What's that smell?' she asked, sniffing.

'It smells like lemons,' Ulf replied.

Tiana perched on the trunk of one of the trees, inspecting its bark. 'Come and see, Ulf. It's lemon moss.'

Ulf walked over to her. The tree trunk was gnarled, and in cracks and crevices in its bark, spongy yellow moss was growing.

Tiana picked a sprig and squeezed it above her mouth. Drops of juice dripped out. 'Mmm. Try it, Ulf. It's refreshing.'

Ulf pulled off a clump of moss and squeezed it. Juice trickled between his knuckles and he licked it off. It tasted just like lemonade.

'Yummy, isn't it?' Tiana said. 'Jungle plants are amazing.' She picked another sprig and put it in her satchel.

Ulf was reaching for more when he noticed a long gash in the bark. 'Look at this, Tiana,' he said. It looked like a claw mark.

'It's huge!' Tiana said. 'What could have made it?'

The gash was deep. Ulf's whole hand fitted inside it. 'What if it was the vampire?' he said.

At that moment, Orson called from up ahead. 'Ulf, there's something here you should see.'

Ulf pushed through the ferns with Tiana flying alongside. He saw Orson and Dr

Fielding kneeling on a bare patch of ground looking at a set of large paw prints. By one print, a single deep hole was gouged.

'These look like the prints of a mono-clawed beast,' Dr Fielding said.

Hurricane Stoat came staggering from behind a clump of ferns with his hand over his mouth. He looked like he was going to be sick. 'I've just seen something awful,' he said.

Ulf stepped through the ferns. On the ground he saw the dead bodies of six adult squealer monkeys. The head of each was missing.

Dr Fielding bent down and touched one of the monkeys. 'The fur's still warm. They can't have been dead long.'

'What could have done this?' Hurricane Stoat asked.

Just then, Ulf heard a grunt. 'Ssh,' he said.

'Hide, everyone,' Orson whispered. They crouched low in the ferns, and Ulf watched as Orson crawled on his belly to the trunk of a buttress tree. The giant peered round it cautiously. 'Blimey,' he whispered.

Ulf crawled to Orson's side and peeked round the trunk. In a clearing beyond the tree, he could see a group of ape-like beasts with shaggy copper-coloured fur. Each had a single large eye, and, on its left front paw, a long hooked claw.

Dr Fielding crept beside Ulf. 'They're cyclapes,' she whispered. The beasts were feeding. Each was holding a monkey head, using its hooked claw to scoop out the brains. 'The largest one on the left is the alpha male,' Dr Fielding whispered. 'He'll be the leader of the group.'

'Drat!' Ulf heard. He glanced back and saw Hurricane Stoat tugging his butterfly net. It was caught on a tree root. 'Blasted trees! They're everywhere,' the photographer said.

'Quiet, Mr Stoat,' Dr Fielding whispered.

Hurricane Stoat yanked the net free then crawled over and squeezed in beside her. 'Sorry,' he said.

But the largest of the cyclapes was already looking in their direction. Ulf saw its big eye staring and quickly jerked his head back, hiding behind the tree. 'I think it might have heard you, Mr Stoat,' he whispered. From the clearing, Ulf heard leaves scrunching.

Tiana flew up, high into the treetop. 'It's coming,' she whispered.

Ulf could feel his heart beating faster. He glanced at Orson. 'What are we going to do?'

The giant winked. 'Mr Stoat, may I borrow your camera?' he asked.

'This isn't a time for photographs,' Hurricane Stoat said.

'Quickly,' Orson told him, lifting the camera from the photographer's neck. 'Dr Fielding, you and Mr Stoat move back a bit, please. Ulf and I will deal with this.'

Dr Fielding led Hurricane Stoat away from the tree to find cover. Ulf pressed his back against the tree trunk. He could hear the cyclape pushing its way nearer.

'Ulf, on the count of three you're going to take its photograph,' Orson whispered, handing him the camera.

'But—'

'One…'

Ulf clutched the camera. He could hear the beast sniffing loudly. It was coming closer.

'Two…'

He heard an angry growl and put his finger on the button.

'Three.'

He jumped out from behind the tree. The beast was right in front of him, staring down with its huge eye. **It lifted its hooked claw ready to strike**. Ulf pointed the camera and pressed the button. As the camera clicked, a bright white light flashed. The beast roared, covering its eye with its paw. It staggered backwards shaking its head from side to side, disorientated by the flash.

'That should buy us some time,' Orson said.

'Now what?'

'Now we run.'

Ulf sprinted off, crashing through the ferns, with the giant striding behind him. They soon caught up with Dr Fielding and Hurricane Stoat, and together they raced through the thick jungle, running between the buttress trees. Tiana flew overhead while Orson stayed at the back, in case the cyclape was following. Ulf tripped, landing face first in a fern.

'Keep up,' Hurricane Stoat said, running past him.

'Are you okay, Ulf?' Tiana called, flying down.

Ulf saw what had tripped him. Lying beside him, among the ferns, was another human skeleton. Its skull was missing.

Tiana saw the skeleton and shivered. 'Urgh, the cyclapes must have got him.'

Beside the headless skeleton, Ulf saw a silver handle. He pulled it from the ferns. 'Look, Tiana, another sword.' Along its blade he read the word: GRENVILLE.

Orson came striding over. 'Up you get, Ulf. We can't hang about.' Then he saw the skeleton and the sword and frowned.

'That's two now,' Ulf said.

Orson took the sword from Ulf. The giant placed it under his boot and bent back its handle, snapping it. 'Let's get out of here,' he said. Orson strode off through the buttress trees, pushing aside the branches like twigs. Ulf and Tiana raced after him as fast as they could, trying to keep up.

'Who are those people, Orson?' Ulf asked. 'And how come they died here?'

'Not now, Ulf,' Orson said, brushing a vine from his face. They hurried beyond the buttress trees, fleeing the cyclapes' territory.

'We should be safe now,' Orson told them, as he clambered through a briar of hookthorn bushes into a grassy glade where two tall gargamast trees had fallen. 'The cyclapes won't follow us this far.'

Dr Fielding and Hurricane Stoat were waiting for them. Dr Fielding was filling her water bottle from a bubbling spring. Hurricane Stoat was hunched over, panting. 'Thank heavens that's over,' he said. 'I thought we were dead meat back there.'

Tiana darted to Dr Fielding. 'Ulf found a skeleton,' she told her.

'Another one?' Dr Fielding asked, screwing the lid back on her bottle.

'With another sword,' Ulf said.

Dr Fielding glanced at Orson. The giant leant down and whispered something in her ear. Ulf saw her frowning. 'Let's hope not, Orson,' she said. Then she turned and headed away along a narrow stream that was trickling from the spring. 'Come on, the river will be this way. We should try to get there before nightfall.'

Ulf looked up. Where the jungle trees had fallen, he could see the sky. The sun was starting to go down. He followed, seeing Orson and Dr Fielding up ahead, whispering to one another. 'Is everything all right?' he called.

'Nothing for you to worry about, Ulf,' Orson called back.

Hurricane Stoat stepped to Ulf's side. 'Did you say you found *another* skeleton? A human skeleton?' he asked nervously.

'Its head was missing,' Ulf said.

Hurricane Stoat rubbed his neck. 'Oh golly.'

Ulf felt Tiana's wings fluttering by his ear. 'I bet he wishes he hadn't come now,' she whispered.

Ulf saw Orson and Dr Fielding trekking

through jungle palms, following the stream. They stopped at a row of imbiber trees. Orson put down his rucksack and parted the branches. 'Look where we are, Ulf,' he called.

Ulf ran to see. Through the trees he glimpsed the red glow of the evening sun reflected on water. A river stretched left and right through the jungle. The stream was flowing into it.

'We'll camp here for the night,' Dr Fielding said. 'Then take to the river in the morning.'

Ulf looked up at Orson. 'Orson, tell me what's going on,' he said.

The giant leant down. 'It's just them skeletons, Ulf. But nothing for y—'

'Orson, can you help me put the hammocks up, please?' Dr Fielding asked. She was unzipping the rucksack.

Orson gave Ulf an awkward smile. 'Right-oh, Dr Fielding,' he said, stepping to help her.

Ulf watched as Orson and Dr Fielding began taking out the hammocks. They knew something, he thought. Something they weren't telling him.

BEASTLY
BUSINESS

CHAPTER EIGHT

That evening, everyone sat around a crackling campfire. It was dark and, through the broken canopy, Ulf could see a thin crescent moon in the sky. The air smelt of sizzling sausages and bubbling baked beans. Dr Fielding was serving food on to metal plates. 'Here you are, Mr Stoat,' she said. 'Eat this. You'll feel better.'

Hurricane Stoat was trembling as he took hold of a plate of food. His eyes were darting left and right. 'Are you sure it's safe here? It's terribly dark.' From the jungle came a hoot. 'The vampire!' the photographer cried, leaping up and spilling his beans.

Orson chuckled. 'That was just a water-owl,

Mr Stoat,' he said. The giant had his boots off and was warming his toes by the fire. 'You'll soon know if a vampire is near. Its screech is hellish frightening.'

Dr Fielding handed a plate to Ulf, and he hungrily shovelled his food in. Between mouthfuls, he glanced at Orson. 'Those skeletons we saw. Were they from the ancient tribe?' he asked.

Orson looked at Dr Fielding then put his plate on the ground. 'No, Ulf. They were slayers,' he said. 'Those swords they had were *slaying* swords.'

'Slayers?' Ulf asked. He didn't understand.

'Vampire slayers,' Orson explained. 'Humans who used to hunt vampires.'

Ulf felt the hairs on his neck stand on end.

'We had no idea that slayers had come to Manchay,' Dr Fielding told him.

There was silence for a moment. Ulf was trying to make sense of it all.

Tiana settled on his shoulder. 'They must have come looking for the jungle vampire,' she whispered.

Ulf could hear the hoots and croaks of the night beasts awake in the jungle. '*When* did they come here?' he asked.

Dr Fielding shrugged. 'We don't know, Ulf. Vampire slayers haven't been heard of since Professor Farraway's time,' she said.

Hurricane Stoat tapped his plate with his fork. 'Do you have any more beans?' he asked. 'And could we please stop talking about vampires and skeletons? It's giving me the heebie-jeebies.'

As Dr Fielding ladled the last of the beans on to Hurricane Stoat's plate, Ulf looked into the flames of the fire.

'Are you okay, Ulf?' Orson asked him.

'What if the slayers found the vampire?' Ulf said. 'What if they killed it?'

The giant poked the fire with a stick. 'Don't worry, Ulf. You saw their skeletons. Those slayers were dead. The jungle beasts got them.'

'Which reminds me, Ulf,' Dr Fielding said. From her pocket, she took out her notepad and turned to the page where she'd sketched the tribal carvings. 'You were right, Ulf. It *was* a map.'

Ulf looked, seeing the vampire at the top of the page and the other carvings drawn below. Dr Fielding pointed to the carving of the mouth surrounded by leaves. 'This marks the snapweed.' She moved her finger to the carving of the eye. 'And this eye must be the cyclapes.'

Ulf remembered the cyclape's big eye staring at him.

'Tomorrow we'll navigate the river,' Dr Fielding said, running her finger up the coiling snake, 'all the way to… here.' She tapped the drawing of the vampire at the top of the page. 'If the vampire's lair is here, we'll find it.'

Ulf smiled at her.

Orson stretched his arms and yawned. 'Well, I think I'll say goodnight now,' he said. He got up and stepped across the fire to a huge hammock held by ropes between two big trees. The trees creaked and bent as the giant got into it.

Hurricane Stoat hurried to the hammock closest to Orson's. 'Bagsy I sleep next to the giant,' he said, trying to climb in.

Ulf and Tiana giggled as Hurricane Stoat fell out the other side.

'You two should get some rest as well,' Dr Fielding told them. 'It's a big day tomorrow.' She was spreading the embers of the fire with a stick, making it safe for the night.

Ulf stood up. 'Goodnight then, Dr Fielding,' he said. 'Thank you for dinner.'

'Sleep well, Ulf,' she replied.

He headed to his hammock, looking forward to spending his first night in the jungle.

* * *

Later that night, Ulf was awake in his hammock. He didn't feel sleepy. He was looking up through the branches when, high in the canopy, he saw a small globe glowing bright silvery-white. It looked like the full moon. *It can't be*, he thought. The full moon was still a whole week away. There was still a week until Ulf would transform from boy to a wolf. He rubbed his eyes and sat up. Then he saw another silvery-white globe appear, then another.

'Pretty, aren't they?' he heard.

Tiana was awake too. She was perched on a branch above him. 'They're flowers, Ulf,' she said. 'They're called moonflowers.'

Ulf stared at the glowing orb-like blooms.

'They open in the moonlight.'

'Tiana, go to sleep,' he heard. It was Dr Fielding calling from her hammock. 'It's late,' she said. 'You need to rest.'

Tiana flew down to Ulf's ear. 'They've got moonjuice in them,' she whispered.

'Tiana, I can still hear you,' Dr Fielding said.

Tiana giggled. 'I'm glad you came, Ulf. Sweet dreams.' And the fairy flew back to her perch.

Ulf liked being on expedition, especially with Tiana. But as he settled down to sleep, he was thinking about the skeletons and the silver slaying swords. He was wondering if the vampire was out there, beyond the river – or whether the slayers had got to it first.

CHAPTER NINE

That same night, Blud and Bone crept through the darkness, following the sound of a stream. Bone had the huge rucksack on his back with a propeller strapped to it and two wing tips sticking from its top. 'I'm worn out,' he complained. 'This thing weighs a tonne.'

Blud stopped beneath a palm tree and peered round its trunk. He saw the faint glowing embers of a campfire. 'There they are,' he whispered.

Around the fire, asleep in their hammocks, were the RSPCB.

Bone dropped his heavy rucksack on the ground. His vest had a long gash torn out of it and he had flying ants in his beard. 'This is stupid,' he said. '**Why are we following them?**'

Above their heads, the leaves of the palm tree rustled. 'Because I said so, you idiots,' a voice hissed.

Blud and Bone peered up into the dark leaves of the palm tree.

'Sorry, Baron Marackai,' Bone said. 'I didn't notice you there.'

The leaves rustled again. 'That's because I'm hiding,' the Baron whispered. 'And so should you be. We don't want them to see us, remember.'

Blud was dabbing his head with a red rag. It was wet with sticky green snapweed juice. 'Begging your pardon, Sir,' he whispered. 'But aren't the RSPCB our enemies?'

'Our *arch* enemies,' the Baron's voice hissed.

'So won't it be difficult to hunt a beast with the RSPCB around?'

'You twit, Blud. Haven't you worked out why they're here? They're looking for the same beast as we are. ALL WE HAVE TO DO IS FOLLOW THEM, AND THEY'LL LEAD US STRAIGHT TO IT.'

'Oh, a *following* plan,' Blud said, sniggering.

Bone glanced up trying to see the Baron. 'And then what, Sir?'

'Then we kill it. And the RSPCB too.'

'Please tell us what beast it is, Sir,' Blud begged.

The leaves shook as the Baron chuckled. 'If I did that, you'd scream with fright. Now keep quiet, and don't let them out of your sight.'

CHAPTER TEN

After breakfast, the RSPCB set off downriver on a large wooden raft. It was built from twelve tree trunks. Orson had gathered them and lashed them together with jungle vine. The giant was kneeling at the back of the raft, using a long branch as a rudder.

Ulf was sitting at the front watching the riverbanks as the raft floated past on the gentle current. The jungle looked different from on the water. Ulf could see the gnarled roots of the imbiber trees drinking from the riverbank, and the beady yellow eyes of mud-rats peering from waterside burrows. The air was cooler out on the river, and he could see the open sky. He watched as a flock of bright-blue gizzard birds flew overhead in a ragged V-formation. A tiger-hawk swooped down plucking a fish from the water.

'This really is a much more pleasant way to see the jungle,' Hurricane Stoat said. The photographer was in the middle of the raft, leaning against his rucksack, fanning himself with his hat.

As the current carried the raft downriver, Ulf saw weedsharks patrolling the shallows, their red fins cutting through the water. Tiana zoomed from the raft following a dragonfly.

'You'll never catch it, Tiana,' Dr Fielding called. She was standing beside Ulf, looking through her binoculars. 'Those things are quick,' she said, smiling at him, then she took her notepad from her pocket and tore out the page where she'd sketched the map. 'Ulf, would you like to be navigator?' she asked, passing it to him.

'I'd love to,' Ulf said, taking the map excitedly.

'It'll be good practice,' Dr Fielding told him.

'One day you might lead your own expedition when you're an RSPCB agent.'

Ulf checked their progress on the map as Orson steered the raft around a bend. They were heading steadily up the snake's tail, moving around a coil.

Travelling by river was much faster than trekking on foot, and there was so much to see. The raft drifted through reeds where tubefish were swimming vertically, camouflaged except for tiny orange fins. Then they floated under a dark tunnel of knotknitters, wiry trees whose branches knotted together in an arch across the water. Orson steered close to the riverbank where rocket-flowers grew, their petals extending like shooting stars. As they journeyed, Dr Fielding peered through her binoculars, pointing out beasts: a walrotter basking on a muddy island, a frill-necked lizaroo snatching an eel from the water and wading kawkaw birds with stilt-like legs spearing fish.

Ulf saw two turtles with shiny golden shells

swim alongside the raft. 'What are those, Dr Fielding?' he asked.

'Those are ore turtles, Ulf. Their shells are made of pure gold, absorbed from sediment in the riverbed.'

Hurricane Stoat had one eye open. His hat was tilted shading his face from the sun. 'Dr Fielding, I'm extremely impressed by your knowledge,' he said. 'How do you know about these beasts?'

'We have records from an expedition of Professor Farraway's,' she explained.

'Professor Farraway? Who's he?'

'He was a great man, Mr Stoat. A pioneer. He was the world's first cryptozoologist, the first to unravel the mysteries of beasts. He once came to Manchay on an expedition.'

Ulf peered into the trees on the shore, imagining the Professor trekking through the jungle years ago. Then he imagined the ancient tribe, thousands of years earlier, living among the beasts. He felt the deck wobble and looked down seeing the water bubbling. The raft was drifting over a shoal of sabre-toothed piranha feeding on the bloated corpse of a crocodon. Orson quickly steered the raft away, around another bend.

Ulf tracked the journey on the map. By the afternoon the raft had made it around three of the snake's coils. They were heading north, deep into Manchay. A pod of marphins, dolphin-like beasts each with a single horn, swam alongside, jumping in the water. Ulf reached out to stroke one, and Hurricane Stoat clicked a photograph.

'Do beasts really need protecting, Dr Fielding?' the photographer asked. 'These all seem fine to me.'

Dr Fielding was dipping a jar over the side of the raft, taking a sample of the river water. 'Today's world is not safe for beasts, Mr Stoat. They need protecting from pollution for example, and global warming and the destruction of their habitats.'

'And hunters,' Ulf added.

Hurricane Stoat looked at Ulf. 'Hunters?' he

asked. 'Surely in this day and age no one would hunt beasts.'

'There's one person who would,' Ulf said.

'Really?' Hurricane Stoat asked. 'And who's that?'

'Marackai,' Ulf said.

'Marackai? What a peculiar name,' Hurricane Stoat remarked.

Marackai was Professor Farraway's son. But unlike the Professor, Marackai hated beasts and hated the RSPCB too. Ulf had fought and defeated him three times.

Tiana flew over and perched on Hurricane Stoat's camera. 'Marackai's horrible,' she whispered. 'His face is twisted like a rotten apple core, and his little finger is missing on his right hand.'

'A missing finger? How unfortunate,' Hurricane Stoat said. He rubbed the little finger on his right hand then gave it a wiggle.

'Marackai's dead, Mr Stoat,' Dr Fielding said. Then she glanced down at Ulf and Tiana and frowned.

'We don't know that for certain,' Ulf said. The last time Ulf had seen Marackai, the hunter was being chased underground by five hungry trolls.

Ulf glanced ahead. The river was widening. He checked the map. They'd passed around four of the snake's coils and were approaching the bulge in its belly where the carving of the pear was drawn. The raft slowed as the water slackened. The river was thick with weed. Ulf could see small trees poking up from the water. Each had a brown stem about a metre tall that was drooping under the weight of a single ripe pear. 'Pears!' Ulf said. 'Look!'

Orson dipped his long branch deep into the water, using it as a paddle. As he rowed through the wide stretch of river, he steered the raft between the pear trees.

'I didn't know pear trees grew in water,' Tiana said.

Hurricane Stoat licked his lips as they passed one of the trees. 'These look jolly tasty,' he said, reaching out to pick a pear.

'I wouldn't touch that if I were you,' Dr Fielding told him.

'But it's only a pear,' the photographer replied. 'What's the harm?'

'You'd be surprised, Mr Stoat,' Orson said. He paddled the raft away from the tree then held out his long branch and gave the pear a knock.

All of a sudden, the water erupted. From under the pear tree leapt an enormous fish with its mouth wide open. The little tree seemed to be growing from its lip. The fish had teeth like splinters and crunched the end of Orson's branch. With a splash, it flopped back down in the water, disappearing under the surface.

'Golly,' Hurricane Stoat said.

A second later, the pear tree bobbed up again, poking from the water just as before.

'It's a bird-catcher,' Orson said, showing Ulf the splintered end of his paddle.

'They're not trees at all,' Dr Fielding explained. 'They're growths on the fishes' mouths designed to attract birds that they then snap and gobble. The pear is bait.'

She glanced at Hurricane Stoat. The photographer was chewing his hat. 'That thing could have bitten me in two,' he gasped.

As Orson steered the raft between the birdcatchers, Ulf looked down trying to glimpse the big fish hiding in the weed below. At the widest point of the river, he noticed something submerged in the weed beneath the surface, something long like a plank of wood. 'Orson, what's that?' he asked, pointing to it.

Orson steered beside it and Ulf could make out a wooden canoe.

'What's a canoe doing here?' Tiana asked.

Inside the canoe, Ulf saw two bony legs. 'There's another skeleton in it,' he said.

'Half a skeleton,' Tiana corrected him.

'Half?' Hurricane Stoat asked.

The upper half of the skeleton was missing.

Tangled in weed at the bottom of the canoe, Ulf spotted another silver sword. 'He must have been another slayer,' he said, reaching down and pulling out the sword to show Orson. On the sword's blade, Ulf read the word: PETERSON.

'He probably tried tasting those pears,' Orson said. The giant took the sword from Ulf and snapped it over his knee. Then he threw the pieces into the river and Ulf saw them glint as they sank. 'He's fish food now,' Orson said. He pushed the canoe down under the weed with his pole, and the bony legs disappeared with it. Then he paddled on, past the last of the birdcatchers, to where the river narrowed again.

Ulf was thinking. 'Dr Fielding, why have those swords got words on them?' he asked.

'They're the names of the families, Ulf,' she said.

'What families?'

'The slayers came from six beast-hunting families. Each family had a silver sword.'

'*Six* families?' Ulf asked.

'The swords were handed down through the generations, from father to son. The slaying continued for hundreds of years.'

'Did you say there were *six* of them?' Ulf asked again. He felt the hairs on his neck standing on end.

'That's right. That sword would have belonged to the Peterson family,' Dr Fielding replied.

Beware the sixth sword, Ulf was thinking. What had the Professor been trying to tell him? He was puzzled, trying to work it out, when he felt the raft moving faster. The current was starting to quicken, sweeping them along.

'Rapids,' Orson called.

Ulf saw frothing white water ahead where the river funnelled between huge rocks. He checked the map. The raft was travelling up the snake's neck. He gripped tightly as it sped along. Dr Fielding crouched beside him. Orson was pushing his branch deep in the water, trying to keep a steady course. Hurricane Stoat was clutching Orson's bootlace. The white water seized hold of the raft and it lurched forwards as the river dropped steeply down. Foaming water splashed over Ulf. Orson was fighting to steer between the rocks, and the raft tossed up and down, careering around bend after bend, faster and faster downriver. Soon, they were approaching the head of the snake. Ulf heard a loud crack as Orson's branch snapped. The raft started spinning out of control.

'Hold tight!' Orson called.

From downriver Ulf could hear a low rumbling noise. It was getting louder. They were hurtling towards a mist of white spray.

'What's that?' Dr Fielding shouted above the noise.

'Waterfall!' Orson boomed. The giant reached over the side of the raft and paddled furiously with his huge hands, trying to steer them to the side of the river. But it was no use. 'Brace yourselves!' he said.

The raft was speeding towards the top of an enormous waterfall. Ulf held his breath.

'We're all going to die!' Hurricane Stoat cried.

Tiana flew into the air.

'Here we go!' Orson called.

The raft shot over the edge of the waterfall and Ulf was flung into the mist of spray. He tumbled through the air, falling head over heels, down and down. It was an almighty drop, and with a big splash he hit the water below. He plunged deep beneath the surface, being pushed down by the force of the waterfall. He tossed and turned, kicking as hard as he could, then bobbed up, gasping for air. Water was crashing down behind him. The noise was deafening. Tree trunks floated around him. The raft was smashed to pieces.

'Are you okay, Ulf?' he heard. He saw Orson swimming over.

Ulf gave a thumbs-up.

Then Dr Fielding popped to the surface. 'Is everyone all right?' she called.

Tiana was circling above. 'Where's Mr Stoat?'

Hurricane Stoat bobbed up last, coughing and spluttering. 'This is a disaster! I'm all wet,' he said. 'Now what are we going to do?'

They were floating in a lake. On the far shore, the sheer rocky side of a mountain loomed over them. Ulf could see jungle at its top. Then he noticed stone steps zigzagging up it. There were hundreds of them. 'That way,' he called, pointing to the steps. He started swimming across the lake and everyone followed. Ulf climbed out at the base of the mountainside and saw that the steep steps were carved into the solid rock. Each looked cracked and worn with age.

Dr Fielding climbed out and stood beside him. 'Incredible,' she said. 'These steps must have been made by the tribe.'

Tiana perched on Dr Fielding's binoculars. 'What for?' she asked.

'They must lead somewhere,' Ulf said. He started climbing up them. 'Let's go and have a look!'

CHAPTER ELEVEN

Climbing high up the cliff steps, Ulf could see out over the jungle, all the way back to the Maripossa Mountains. The sun was setting and the horns of Manchay were tinted red in the evening light. He'd travelled a long way, he realised.

As he reached the trees at the top of the cliff, the steps became shallower, turning into a stone path that sloped up into jungle.

Ulf stopped and stared in astonishment, seeing large stone statues lining either side of the pathway. Each was of a beast, huge and chiselled with cold stone eyes. He stepped slowly forwards, passing a statue of a spined mammoth, then a four-legged fish. He passed a statue of a gorillax and one of a scorpius. In the dim light he saw more up ahead: the warty face of a giant toad, a long-beaked razorbird and others with huge wings, hooked claws and horned heads.

Tiana came zooming over his shoulder. 'Wow, look at all these,' she said, sparkling.

Ulf turned, hearing Orson's heavy boots coming up the steps. The giant peered through the trees. 'Blimey,' he said.

Dr Fielding stepped out from behind him and saw the lines of statues. 'How extraordinary,' she said. She trod slowly along the gloomy path, glancing at each statue in turn.

Orson was waiting for Hurricane Stoat to make his way up the steps. 'Get your camera ready,' the giant said. 'You're going to love this.'

Hurricane Stoat came puffing through the trees. His rucksack was slung over his shoulder and he was fanning himself with his hat. 'I... counted... over... six... hundred... steps.' He saw the large beasts either side of him. 'Run for your lives!' he cried.

Orson took hold of his arm. 'There's no need to be afraid, Mr Stoat. They're only statues.'

Hurricane Stoat glanced around the gloomy jungle path, checking more closely. 'Yes, well. It's hard to tell in this light,' he said, embarrassed.

'What *is* this place, Dr Fielding?' Ulf asked.

'It looks to me like some kind of processional route,' she replied. 'Whatever it is, it must have been an important place for the tribe to have built these statues.'

Ulf followed her up the path past a statue of a hydra with eight stone heads then past a throttle-neck serpent coiled around a crocodon. In the dim light, the stone beasts looked almost real.

There was a flash of light. Ulf looked back and saw Hurricane Stoat taking photographs. Orson was leaning against the statue of the gorillax with his elbow on its shoulder, smiling.

'That'll be a superb picture,' Hurricane Stoat said.

Orson stepped beside Ulf. 'Will you take one of me and Ulf together?' he asked.

Hurricane Stoat clicked his camera, photographing the two of them beside a stone walrotter.

'What *are* all these beasts, Orson?' Ulf asked. There were many he didn't recognise.

'They're all jungle beasts, Ulf,' the giant said. He pointed up the path to a statue of a clawed lizard. 'That's a crane-claw. They're extinct now.'

Suddenly Ulf heard a loud cry from behind him: 'Help!'

He looked back. Hurricane Stoat had vanished. 'Mr Stoat? Mr Stoat, where are you?'

Dr Fielding came running down the path. 'What's wrong?' she asked. 'I heard a cry.'

'Hurricane Stoat's disappeared,' Ulf told her.

'He was with us a second ago,' Orson said, looking puzzled.

Ulf checked behind statues and peered into the dark jungle. Suddenly, he heard a deep croak. He glanced up and saw the statue of the warty toad looking down at him. It blinked. *Uh-oh*, he thought. 'Dr Fielding, this one's not a st—' But before Ulf could finish his sentence,

a long tongue whipped from the toad's mouth. It coiled around him, snatching him upwards, pulling him between the toad's fat lips. 'Help!' he called, as he was sucked inside into darkness.

Ulf was trapped in the toad's mouth. He heard a loud squelch as the toad gulped and sent him tumbling backwards down a dark tube. He was sliding down its throat. He landed knee-deep in warm sticky juice. It sloshed and echoed. He was in some kind of dark chamber.

'Who goes there?' he heard. It was the voice of Hurricane Stoat.

'Mr Stoat? It's me, Ulf. Where are you?'

Ulf heard the sound of a zip, then a click as a light came on. He saw Hurricane Stoat shining a torch, sitting in the juices with his rucksack beside him.

'It stinks in here,' Hurricane Stoat said.

In the torchlight, Ulf saw fleshy walls rippling around them. Two dead parrots and three drowned rats floated around his knees.

They were inside the toad's stomach. At that moment, Ulf heard a sound like a running tap.

'What's that noise?' Hurricane Stoat whispered.

From the top of the chamber, more juices were flowing in.

'It's gastric juice,' Ulf said. 'The toad's digesting.'

'Digesting what?' Hurricane Stoat asked nervously.

'Us,' Ulf replied.

Hurricane Stoat crawled through the contents of the stomach. He gripped Ulf's leg. 'Please save me,' he said. 'I'm too young to die.'

Just then, Ulf heard a voice coming from beyond the stomach wall: 'Ulf, are you in there?' It was Dr Fielding.

'We're trapped,' Ulf called.

'You're stuck in a gorge toad,' he heard. 'Listen carefully. I'll try to help you get out.'

Ulf pressed his ear to the slimy stomach wall.

'Look up and find the hole where you came in,' Dr Fielding called. 'That's the pyloric sphincter. Reach into it as far as you can and feel for a rubbery lump of skin.'

Hurricane Stoat shone his torch upwards,

lighting the stomach's fleshy ceiling. In its middle Ulf saw a small opening with skin pinched around it. He reached up, squeezing his fingers into the opening. It widened and he slid his hand in. Slime ran down his arm. 'I can't feel anything,' he called.

'Keep trying,' Dr Fielding called back.

Ulf stepped on to Hurricane Stoat's rucksack. He reached higher, pushing his hand up to his elbow. Then he stood on tiptoe, sliding his arm right up to his shoulder. He felt something rubbery. 'I've got it,' he called. It felt like a lump of meat.

'That's the toad's epiglottis, Ulf,' he heard. 'Try pulling on it.'

Ulf pulled on the dangling flesh. There was a loud rumble and all at once the contents of the stomach welled up around him.

'Aaaargh!' Hurricane Stoat cried.

The stomach walls were squeezing inwards. The pyloric sphincter stretched wide and Ulf and Hurricane Stoat were thrust upwards in a torrent of juice. They shot up the toad's throat and burst out of its mouth. They landed on the path with a squelch, gastric juices gushing over them, along with half-digested birds and rats.

Ulf heard Tiana giggling. She was sparkling above him, pinching her nose. 'You stink,' she said. By Tiana's light, Ulf saw Orson and Dr Fielding peering down at him.

'Expertly done, Ulf,' Dr Fielding told him.

Ulf glanced up at the toad. It belched.

'Gorge toads are greedy creatures,' Orson said. The giant stroked the toad's head. 'They're friendly though. Too fat to hop.'

Hurricane Stoat was shaking the sick from his torch. 'It's broken,' he said. 'Those juices have *melted* my torch.'

Ulf and Hurricane Stoat stood up, dripping with vomit. Orson handed Ulf a giant-sized handkerchief from his pocket. It was as big as a towel. 'You two might want to wipe that lot off,' he said. 'Before it dissolves your clothes.'

'And then we should get going,' Dr Fielding added. 'It's nearly dark.'

As Ulf wiped himself clean with the giant's

handkerchief he noticed a glint of silver by his foot. He bent down. In the pool of sick was a silver sword. Ulf pulled it out. Engraved on its blade was the word: HARRISON.

'How did that sword get there?' Tiana asked.

'It came out of the toad's stomach,' Ulf said.

Orson took the sword. 'The toad must have digested a slayer.'

'What a horrible way to go,' Hurricane Stoat remarked as Orson snapped the sword in two.

'That's four dead slayers now,' Ulf said. *Two to go*, he thought as they headed off up the path.

Dr Fielding handed out torches. 'Here you are, Mr Stoat, have a new one.' She was leading the way between the statues, through the tunnel of trees. The path climbed gently upwards. Then, after a hundred metres or so, quite suddenly, it stopped. In front of them was a thick curtain of vines.

'Oh, dear, a dead end,' Hurricane Stoat said. 'Well at least we can say we *tried* to find that vampire. Shall we head back now?'

Ulf parted the vines and pointed his torch

into the dark jungle beyond. His torch beam shone on gnarled and twisted trees. It lit up a slab of rock sticking from the ground. He saw more slabs standing vertically, overgrown with creepers. In front of each was a low mound.

Dr Fielding stepped beside him. '*Of course*,' she muttered. 'Ulf, do you recognise this place?'

Ulf remembered the photograph he'd seen in Professor Farraway's expedition file. 'Gravestones,' he said.

'That's right, Ulf. It's a burial ground. This is the burial ground of the ancient tribe. It's no wonder they carved that map.'

'What do you mean?' Ulf asked her.

'This would have been a sacred place for the tribe. The map's been leading us here all along.'

Ulf thought for a second. 'But what about the vampire?' he asked. 'It had the vampire carved on it too.'

'Just keep your eyes peeled,' Dr Fielding said.

Hurricane Stoat gulped loudly. 'Please don't tell me we're going in there.'

CHAPTER TWELVE

Ulf pushed aside the vines and stepped into the burial ground. He shone his torch among the gravestones. Some were virtually hidden, bound by creepers and scabbed with moss. There was a chill in the air and he could feel the hairs on his bare arms standing on end.

'It's so cold here,' Tiana said. Her wing tips were shivering.

Ulf felt a gust of freezing-cold air rise up through him, then he heard a faint rustling of leaves overhead. He shone his torch into the branches and saw a ghostly black face with empty eyes. 'Look,' he whispered.

'Eeek,' Tiana shrieked.

Ulf felt Hurricane Stoat grip his shoulder. 'W-what *is* that?' the photographer stuttered.

Dr Fielding and Orson crouched in the dark.

'It's an encanto,' Dr Fielding whispered. She swept her torch beam around the burial ground. 'Look, there are more.'

Ulf saw more encantos drifting like black smoke in a breeze. They were rising from the ground and gliding through the trees. Each had haunting, empty eyes.

'Encantos? What the heck are encantos?' Hurricane Stoat asked.

'They're the spirits of the ancient tribe,' Dr Fielding explained. 'They haunt the jungle.'

'You mean they're g-g-ghosts?'

'They're good ghosts,' Ulf told him. 'The tribe used to live with the beasts.'

Ulf trod carefully, following Orson and Dr Fielding through the burial ground, trying not to disturb the graves. He could see slabs of stone as far as his torch beam shone. The burial ground seemed never-ending.

'Wait for me,' Hurricane Stoat called. Ulf

looked round and shone his torch. The photographer was taking his butterfly net from his rucksack. He crept to Ulf's side, prodding the encantos as he passed. 'Shoo. Keep away,' he said.

'It's okay, Mr Stoat. They're not hurting us,' Ulf said.

'But they're ghosts!' the photographer replied.

'Come on, or we'll get left behind,' Ulf said, stepping over a grave. Orson and Dr Fielding were up ahead in the darkness.

Ulf shone his torch to light the way. Suddenly, it lit a frosty white face.

'What's that?' Hurricane Stoat whispered, seeing it.

The face looked human. It had a white beard and its mouth was open as if it was screaming, but it was making no sound. Ulf ran the beam of his torch downwards, and saw the frosted figure of a man standing among the graves. Hurricane Stoat gasped. In the man's hand, pointing towards them, was a silver sword.

'It's another slayer,' Ulf said.

'Keep away from us!' Hurricane Stoat ordered

the man. But the man wasn't moving. He looked frozen, icy white, and there were thin cracks over him. Ulf slowly crept towards him.

'Careful now,' Hurricane Stoat said.

Ulf reached out to touch the man. He felt as cold as ice. He was frozen solid. Ulf tapped him. 'He's dead.'

Tiana came sparkling through the trees. 'There you are,' she said. She saw the icy slayer and stopped. 'Urgh, what happened to him?'

'It looks like he caught a chill,' Hurricane Stoat said.

Ulf was staring at the sword in the frozen slayer's hand. Engraved along its blade he read the word: DE MONTFORD. 'Quick, Tiana, go and fetch Orson.'

Ulf prised the sword from the slayer and the man's hand snapped off with it.

'Eeeyugh!' Tiana said. She quickly flew off to find the giant.

Suddenly, Ulf heard a sound like the wind whistling. It was encantos. Their black shadows were gathering all around him.

'Clear off! Go away!' Hurricane Stoat said, waving his net at them.

Ulf felt the air turning icy cold as the encantos grew in number. They began circling around him, eyeing the sword.

'What are they doing?' Hurricane Stoat asked. He grabbed the sword from Ulf and pointed it at them. 'Don't come any closer. I'm not afraid to use this.' The photographer began swiping the sword at the encantos, but its blade passed straight through them. It was useless. They circled faster, their hollow eyes staring.

'Stop it, Mr Stoat, you're making them angry,' Ulf told him.

'I'm protecting us,' Hurricane Stoat said. The sword was shaking in his hands.

Ulf reached for its handle to take it back, but Hurricane Stoat wouldn't let go. The encantos whirled like a fierce black storm.

'Ulf, where are you?' Ulf heard. It sounded like Orson, but he couldn't see the giant. Ulf was trapped in a freezing black cloud of

encantos. He could feel a biting chill. His arms and legs were going numb as the air grew colder. His skin was stiffening and turning frosty. Ice crystallized on the hairs on his arms.

'What's-s-s h-h-happening?' Hurricane Stoat shivered.

They were being frozen alive.

'Dr-dr-drop the s-sword, Mr Stoat. It's the sword that's making them angry.' Ulf wrenched the sword from Hurricane Stoat's grasp and threw it to the ground.

As he did, the whirlwind began to slow. The encantos started peeling away, drifting into the trees. Ulf and Hurricane Stoat stood shivering from the cold. Ulf's whole body felt numb and rigid. Hurricane Stoat had an icicle hanging from his nose.

Tiana flew to Ulf, with Orson and Dr Fielding following. 'Are you okay?' the fairy asked.

'I th-th-think so,' Ulf said, shivering.

She blasted Ulf's skin with hot sparkles.

'Those things n-nearly k-k-killed us,' Hurricane Stoat said, trembling.

'Blankets, Orson,' Dr Fielding said.

Orson took off his rucksack and pulled out two blankets. Dr Fielding wrapped them around Ulf and Hurricane Stoat. 'These will warm you up,' she said, rubbing Ulf's shoulders and back. He felt himself thawing.

Orson stood by the rigid slayer. With one finger, he gave him a poke and the slayer toppled to the ground, smashing like ice.

'It was the encantos, Orson,' Ulf said. 'They must have killed him. They're icy cold.'

Dr Fielding wiped the frost from Ulf's hair. 'You don't want to mess with encantos,' she said. 'They're the protectors of the jungle. They can breathe death.'

Orson picked up the sword and snapped it in two. 'At least that's the last of these.'

Ulf thought back, counting the swords: PILKINGTON, GRENVILLE, PETERSON, HARRISON, DE MONTFORD. 'But that's only five swords,' he said. 'You said there were six.'

'That's right, Ulf,' Dr Fielding told him. 'But the sixth sword won't be in the jungle.'

'Why not?'

'Because the sixth sword belonged to Professor Farraway,' she replied.

'The Professor?' Ulf said, confused. 'Why did *he* have it?'

'Hang on,' Hurricane Stoat said. 'I thought you said Professor Farraway *liked* beasts. You mean to say that *he* was a slayer too?'

'No, *he* wasn't a slayer,' Dr Fielding replied. 'But his ancestors were. The Farraway family were notorious beast hunters. When the Professor inherited the Farraway sword, he stopped the family slaying.'

'See, Ulf. I told you there was no need to worry,' Tiana whispered.

No sooner had she spoken than a piercing screech sounded over the jungle. It sent tingles up and down Ulf's spine. He shuddered in his blanket and his hair stood on end as he looked up into the treetops. He couldn't stop shaking. **It was the most frightening sound imaginable, like the cry of approaching death.**

CHAPTER THIRTEEN

'Get under cover,' Dr Fielding said. 'Lights off.'

Ulf dashed beneath the leafy cover of a bullberry tree and crouched beside Dr Fielding, wrapped in his blanket. His heart was thumping. The screech was unlike anything he'd ever heard – it was as if his ear drums had been pierced by a needle. He could still hear them ringing. 'Was that what I think it was?' he whispered.

'It's here somewhere, Ulf,' Dr Fielding said. 'That was the cry of a vampire.'

Orson stooped under the bullberry's branches. 'It's probably out hunting,' he whispered.

Hurricane Stoat clutched the giant's leg. 'Please don't let it bite me.'

'It's all right, Mr Stoat. You'll be safe here,' Orson told him. 'This bullberry tree will conceal you from above.' The tree had thick broad leaves and large purple berries.

'We should try to get a visual on it, Orson,' Dr Fielding whispered. 'See if we can find its lair.' She turned to Ulf. 'Ulf, I'd like you to stay here with Tiana and Mr Stoat.'

'But can't I come with you?' he asked. Ulf wanted to see the vampire for himself.

'I'm serious, Ulf. Stay hidden until we've checked things out,' Dr Fielding told him.

'We may be gone a while,' Orson said. Then he leant down and whispered in Ulf's ear: 'We need you to look after Mr Stoat. He's a bit jumpy.'

Hurricane Stoat was trembling in his blanket.

'Are you ready, Orson?' Dr Fielding asked.

Orson picked a bunch of berries and popped them in his mouth. 'Ready,' he replied.

'Good luck,' Ulf said, as Orson and Dr Fielding headed off through the trees.

'This is madness,' Hurricane Stoat said. 'How can they just leave us here alone?'

'You're not alone, Mr Stoat,' Tiana told him. 'Ulf and I are with you.'

'It's okay for you. No vampire's going to waste its time on a thimbleful of *fairy* blood.'

'Ssh,' Ulf said. 'Dr Fielding told us to keep quiet.' He was listening for the vampire.

Tiana nestled into his pocket, and Ulf huddled under his blanket, with Hurricane Stoat whimpering beside him. Ulf felt excited and terrified all at once, wondering if the beast was overhead. They waited in silence for Orson and Dr Fielding to return. The minutes turned into hours and the hours stretched on and on.

'Where have they got to?' Hurricane Stoat asked. 'Are they just going to leave us here all night? What on earth's keeping them?' He nibbled his fingernails impatiently.

'I'm sure they won't be too much longer,' Ulf reassured him. But by the middle of the night, Dr Fielding and Orson still weren't back. Hurricane Stoat had fallen asleep. He was wrapped in his blanket, snoring. Ulf didn't feel tired. His mind was wandering, thinking back to the swords. Something still didn't make sense. Why would Professor Farraway warn him about the sixth sword if the Professor had it himself?

Ulf was trying to fathom it all when, from the darkness, he heard a *hissssssssss*.

'What was that?' Tiana asked, poking her head from his pocket.

Ulf looked up and saw the glistening scales of a throttle-neck serpent. It was uncoiling from a branch above, sliding downwards and flicking out its tongue. It licked Hurricane Stoat's cheek.

Hurricane Stoat snorted and opened his eyes.

'Move away very slowly,' Ulf said.

'Snake!' Hurricane Stoat shrieked, seeing the throttle-neck serpent. 'It bit me!' He leapt up, fumbling for his torch. He shone the light in the serpent's eyes and it hissed again.

'Calm down, Mr Stoat,' Ulf whispered. 'Throttle-necks don't bite. They crush.' He edged away slowly as the serpent's tail sneaked down and wrapped around Hurricane Stoat's torch. The light went out with a crunch.

'I'm not staying here!' Hurricane Stoat cried. He ran from the bullberry tree, calling into the darkness: 'Mr Orson, where are you?'

Ulf sprinted after him. 'Come back, Mr Stoat!'

Tiana flew from Ulf's pocket. 'Stop, Ulf!' she said. 'The vampire, remember?'

Ulf was running, following the sound of Hurricane Stoat crashing through the undergrowth. He leapt over gravestones, feeling icy chills as he ran through encantos. He pushed aside vines and ducked under branches.

'Ulf, we're supposed to stay undercover,' Tiana said, weaving alongside him.

But Ulf could hear Mr Stoat running in the darkness. 'Mr Stoat, come back!' he called.

Suddenly, a spine-tingling screech echoed above the trees.

'Get down!' Tiana cried.

Ulf dived to the ground and Tiana landed beside him. His heart was beating quickly. 'Mr Stoat, are you safe?' he called.

But there was no reply.

CHAPTER FOURTEEN

Meanwhile, at the entrance to the burial ground, Blud and Bone were peering through the curtain of vines. They were soaking wet and their clothes were torn.

'W-w-what was that noise?' Blud whispered, clutching Bone's leg.

'My ears hurt,' Bone replied, trembling.

'Turn your torch on,' Blud told him.

'Don't you dare,' a voice hissed. It was the voice of Baron Marackai.

'Baron? Where are you?' Blud asked, looking into the darkness.

'I'm hiding, you fool,' the Baron said. His voice came from behind a gravestone. 'What you just heard was the cry of a beast. *Our* beast.'

'Please, Sir. W-what beast is it?' Blud asked, nervously.

'It sounded scary, Sir,' Bone said.

The Baron laughed. 'That was the cry of a *vampire*.'

'A v-v-vampire!' Blud and Bone both said. They hugged one another tightly.

'Stop that, you ninnies,' the Baron ordered.

'But, Sir, vampires are d-d—'

'Shut up!' the Baron said. 'I told you you'd be afraid.' He cackled. 'Well don't just stand there like dummies. In you come.'

Blud and Bone shuffled forwards through the vines.

'That's it. And a bit further.'

Blud and Bone shuffled again. They stood by a grave, shaking.

'Now get to work, you scaredy cats. Prepare the flying machine.'

CHAPTER FIFTEEN

'Do you think Mr Stoat's all right?' Tiana whispered. 'What if the vampire got him?'

They were creeping through the jungle, searching for Hurricane Stoat.

'Why did he have to run off?' Tiana asked. 'Now we're lost, and Orson and Dr Fielding are probably looking for us.'

'It'll be morning soon,' Ulf said. He was looking up through the broken canopy. In a treetop he glimpsed a glowing silver flower. 'Look, Tiana, a moonflower. Like the ones we saw last night.' It was high up, growing in a nook between the branches.

Ulf felt Tiana's wings fluttering by his ear.

'There'll be moonjuice inside it, Ulf,' she whispered.

'What's moonjuice?' he asked her.

'You can drink it, Ulf. You'd like it.'

Ulf noticed the flower's silver petals closing as the moon went down. Quickly, he started climbing the tree to take a closer look. He pulled himself up through the branches, holding on to vines as he went.

'Ulf, stay hidden,' Tiana called.

But Ulf ignored her. He climbed higher then shuffled along a branch to see inside the flower.

Tiana flew up after him. 'Ulf, we're meant to be hiding from the vampire.'

'I just want to take a quick look,' Ulf said. He was stretching to peer inside the moonflower when he heard a flapping sound above the trees. It sounded like wings beating overhead. 'Tiana, can you hear that?' he whispered.

'Uh-oh,' the fairy said.

Suddenly, Ulf heard branches snapping and the tree shook. From above, a huge black beast with red eyes came crashing towards him. 'It's the vampire!' he cried. Ulf gripped a vine and leapt from the branch. He swung through the darkness, hearing the vampire smashing branches, coming after him. He grabbed hold of another vine, swinging like a monkey through the trees.

'Quickly, Ulf. It's following!' Tiana called. She was flying ahead of him, sparkling.

Ulf glanced back and saw the vampire's red eyes glowing. He reached for another vine, trying to get away. As he grabbed it, the vine snapped and he tumbled through the branches, landing on the ground with a thud. He was lying on a grave.

The huge silhouette of the vampire loomed over him from the trees, its red eyes staring. He could see two long white fangs, glinting.

'Ulf, get up!' Tiana cried.

The vampire screeched and a shockwave shuddered through Ulf. He covered his ears.

'Get up, Ulf!'

He saw the vampire's huge black wings opening. The branches around it were snapping.

It screeched again. Then all of a sudden it took off from the trees, flying back into the sky.

Ulf staggered to his feet. 'What happened, Tiana?' he asked. Through the leaves, he saw thin rays of light filtering down. Dawn was breaking over the jungle.

'You were lucky, Ulf. It must have seen the light,' Tiana said. 'It'll be heading back to its lair.'

Ulf could hear the vampire's wings beating overhead as it flew away above the jungle. 'Come on, let's follow it.'

'Follow it? Ulf, no, that's crazy!' Tiana told him.

But Ulf was already running off through the jungle. 'Dr Fielding wants to know where its lair is,' he called. He leapt over gravestones and weaved through the trees, following the sound of the vampire's wings beating overhead. His bare feet were slipping on moss and kicking through creepers. The ground was sloping upwards, steeper and steeper.

The trees thinned and all of a sudden the ground dropped away in front of him. Ulf grabbed hold of a branch to stop himself falling into a vast black crater. It was huge – an enormous hole in the middle of the jungle. It must have been nearly a hundred metres wide and looked deep and dark. He heard a screech echo inside it as the vampire dived down to its gloomy depths.

'What *is* this place?' Tiana asked, hovering beside him.

Ulf was looking down into the crater. In the half-light of dawn, he could see only shadows at its bottom. Then he heard a booming voice calling him. 'Is that you, Ulf?'

He looked over. At the top of the crater, on its far side, he saw the tall silhouette of Orson. The giant came striding around the crater's rim towards him. 'Ulf, Tiana? Are you all right?'

Ulf saw Dr Fielding and Hurricane Stoat running behind the giant. All three were hurrying. 'We're fine,' he called back.

As they came nearer, Ulf pointed into the crater. 'The vampire's down there,' he said.

'We've been looking for you,' Orson said, stepping to Ulf's side.

Dr Fielding and Hurricane Stoat arrived a few moments later. 'Mr Stoat's been worried about you,' Dr Fielding said, panting. 'He said you ran off in the night.'

'We never!' Tiana said. '*He* was the one who got scared!'

Hurricane Stoat glanced sheepishly at Dr Fielding. 'Maybe I did get a bit spooked,' he said.

Orson smiled at Ulf and Tiana. 'I knew you two could take care of yourselves.' Then he glanced down into the crater. 'So you found the vampire's lair?'

Dr Fielding peered over the crater's edge. 'It's an extinct volcano, by the looks of things,' she told them. 'I suggest we get a few hours' rest and then go down there.'

'Go down?' Hurricane Stoat asked. 'Into that great big hole? With a vampire?'

'Yes,' Dr Fielding said. 'I'd like to see this beast close up.'

BEASTLY
BUSINESS

CHAPTER SIXTEEN

It was midday and, after a few hours' sleep, the RSPCB were ready to get going. Orson tied one end of a climbing rope around a tree trunk and threw the other end over the crater's edge. 'I'll climb down first,' he said, hoisting the rucksack on to his back. 'See you at the bottom.'

Ulf, Dr Fielding and Hurricane Stoat watched as the giant gripped the rope and leaned back over the rim of the crater. The rope creaked under his weight.

'I hope it's tied well,' Hurricane Stoat said. 'That looks an awfully long way to fall.'

Ulf looked down into the crater. Far below,

he could see the bottom strewn with rocks. Ulf watched Orson abseiling down.

'You can go next, Ulf,' Dr Fielding said.

Ulf waited for Orson to reach the bottom. The giant took a quick look around then gave a thumbs-up. 'Down you come,' he called.

Ulf held the rope and leaned backwards over the edge. He lowered himself down, his bare feet against the crater wall. The rock felt hot where the sun had warmed it. He could see tree roots poking from it, and lizards peering from cracks. It was a long way down, and as he descended, he noticed flies buzzing in the air around him. There were more of them the lower he went.

When Ulf reached the bottom, he stepped down and his foot squished on something furry. He hopped to one side and saw that he'd trodden on the rotting carcass of a squealer monkey.

'Vampire food,' Orson said to him.

The monkey's body was saggy and shapeless, and swarming with flies. It had two large holes in its chest where sharp fangs had pierced it.

'Go away,' Ulf heard. He glanced up and saw Tiana flying towards him, shooing flies with her sparkles. She was pinching her nose. 'It smells down here,' she said.

The air was heavy with the stench of rotting flesh. Ulf looked around the crater and saw the carcasses of other jungle beasts scattered among the rocks. There were crocodons, hammer-headed eagles and giant sloths, their skins saggy and their bodies drained of blood. 'Where's the vampire, Orson?' he asked.

'My guess is it's in there,' the giant said, pointing along the wall of the crater.

Ulf looked over to a jagged opening where the rock had split. The ground outside was littered with carcasses. 'Can I take a look?' he asked.

'Wait, Ulf,' Tiana said. 'It could be dangerous.'

Orson looked up at the sun. 'It's okay, Tiana. The vampire will be fast asleep now. It won't wake up in the daytime.'

While Orson waited for Dr Fielding and Hurricane Stoat to climb down, Ulf crept quietly along the wall of the crater and peered into the opening in the rock. It was gloomy inside. He stepped in over bones and found himself in a tall dark cave.

'I can't see,' Tiana whispered to him. She turned on her sparkles, and Ulf gasped. At the back of the cave, hanging upside-down from the ceiling, was the huge black shape of the jungle vampire. It was sleeping.

Ulf stepped towards it.

'Careful, Ulf,' Tiana whispered, fearing the vampire might wake up.

Ulf hesitated. But the vampire wasn't moving. Its wings were folded around its body and its eyes were shut.

'It's a beauty, isn't it?' he heard from behind him. Ulf looked round and saw Orson peering in through the opening to the cave. Dr Fielding and Hurricane Stoat were beside him.

'How wonderful,' Dr Fielding said, stepping inside. 'This is the largest vampire I've ever seen. Look at its fangs. They're huge.' She stepped towards the beast and glanced up and down its enormous body. 'It must be four metres tall.'

'Dr Fielding, are you sure this is safe?' Hurricane Stoat asked, peering from behind Orson's leg.

'Vampires are strictly night hunters, Mr Stoat,' Dr Fielding told him. 'During the day they shut down completely. It's a state known as necro-somnia. It's perfectly safe.' She touched one of the vampire's fangs. 'Orson, can you set up the lamp so we can get a better look at it?'

Orson put down his rucksack and took out a tall lamp on a tripod.

'You can touch it too, if you want, Ulf,' Dr Fielding said. 'It won't wake up.'

Ulf placed his hand on the vampire's cheek, feeling its bristly hairs and wrinkled skin. The vampire felt cold. He touched one of its fangs and the tip felt sharp. 'It's not breathing,' he said.

Dr Fielding knelt beside Ulf. 'While a vampire sleeps, its vital functions switch off to conserve energy,' she told him.

A soft glow lit up the cave as Orson switched on the lamp. Now Ulf could see every detail of the vampire: its wrinkled eyelids and red stains on its fangs. Around its mouth was black hair, matted with blood. He saw its long pointy bat-like ears, and its large leathery wings. It was gripping the roof of the cave with gnarled black claws.

From the rucksack Dr Fielding took out her medical box. She placed it on the ground beside the vampire and opened its lid. Inside, Ulf saw hypodermic needles, test-tubes, specimen jars, weighing scales, a measuring tape and tools for probing and prodding. She took out a pair of tweezers and plucked a hair from the vampire's cheek.

'Why are you doing that?' Hurricane Stoat asked from the entrance to the cave.

'When we get back to headquarters, I'll run DNA tests in the lab to determine the vampire's genetic code,' Dr Fielding said, popping the hair into a specimen bag. 'This is an entirely new species of vampire, unique to this habitat. It's without doubt one of the most important crypto-zoological discoveries of modern times.'

'If you're all right in here, Dr Fielding, I

think I'll check out the crater,' Orson said. 'See what else lives round here.'

'Good idea,' Dr Fielding replied. 'See what scavenger beasts there are.'

Tiana was perched on Ulf's shoulder. The little fairy had her hand over her nose and mouth. She took off, flying after the giant. 'Wait for me, Orson. I'm coming with you,' she called. 'It stinks of blood in here.'

Ulf watched as Dr Fielding pushed her hands between the vampire's lips. 'Okay, Ulf, let's get a better look at this beast.' She pulled its lips apart and Ulf saw the full length of its two white fangs. They were each as long as his forearm and as sharp as knives.

'Aren't they magnificent?' Dr Fielding said. 'Easily the biggest fangs of any vampire I've seen. Can you help me, Ulf?'

Ulf gripped the vampire's lip, pulling it down. It felt cold and wet. The beast's mouth gave off the strong acrid smell of blood. He looked inside it and saw the vampire's tongue wet with bloody saliva and glistening in the lamplight.

From her medical box, Dr Fielding took out a spatula and a test-tube, and took a sample of its saliva. 'When vampires feed, Ulf, an enzyme in their saliva stops the blood of their prey from clotting,' she said. 'It means they can keep the blood flowing even if their prey has died.'

Dr Fielding put the saliva sample into her medical box then took out a measuring tape. She held it up to one of the fangs. 'Forty-two centimetres,' she read. Then she measured the shorter teeth on the vampire's lower jaw. 'These teeth here are the grinding teeth, Ulf,' she explained. 'When vampires close their mouths, the grinding teeth rub against the fangs keeping them nice and sharp.' The grinding teeth were rough like sandpaper. 'Mr Stoat, could you take a picture of this, please?'

Hurricane Stoat stepped into the cave holding his camera. His hand was shaking, his fingers twitching.

'Are you okay?' Ulf asked him.

'Just a little nervous,' the photographer said. He gripped his left hand over his right, stopping

it from shaking, and held his camera up to take a picture. 'Smile,' he said. The camera flashed. 'My, what a gruesome-looking beast that is!'

'Vampires may not be pretty,' Dr Fielding said. 'But they're among the most remarkable predators on Earth. Every part of their anatomy is perfectly adapted for nocturnal hunting.'

She shone her torch at one of the vampire's long ears. The skin was wrinkled and hairy. At the bottom of the ear Ulf saw thick muscle. 'Vampires' ears are hinged at their base, Ulf. They can swivel to pick up sounds from any direction. It helps them hone in on their prey.'

Ulf thought back to being up in the treetop and how the vampire had attacked as if from nowhere. He hadn't told Dr Fielding what had happened. She'd only get worried.

Dr Fielding opened one of the vampire's eyelids. Hundreds of tiny red blood vessels criss-crossed the eyeball. Ulf watched as the eyeball slowly started glowing.

'Run! It's waking up!' Hurricane Stoat cried, dashing from the cave.

'Don't worry, Mr Stoat, it's only a reaction to the light,' Dr Fielding called. She turned to Ulf. 'Vampires' eyeballs act like prisms, trapping any available light inside them. It helps them see when they're hunting in the dark.' She let go of the eyelid and it gently closed again. 'Ulf, could you carefully pull its left wing open for me, now?'

Hurricane Stoat peered back in the entrance as Ulf and Dr Fielding each took hold of a wing. They pulled them outwards and the wings unfolded like huge black sails, stretching all the way to the walls of the cave. Each wing had five long bones running across it to five single claws that were spread along its lower edge. Ulf had never seen wings that had claws.

'In essence, these wings are enormous webbed hands, Ulf,' Dr Fielding said. 'The long wing bones are the equivalent of fingers.' She pulled on the wing membrane and it stretched like elastic. 'This membrane allows the vampire to flex its wings into different shapes when it's flying. Vampires are more manoeuvrable than other winged beasts. It's an advantage when hunting prey.'

Ulf touched the wing membrane. It felt thin and stretchy like rubber. He rubbed his fingers. 'It's waxy,' he said.

'That's a natural oil,' Dr Fielding said. 'To protect it from the elements.' She scraped a sample of the wax into a specimen jar and placed it in her medical box. 'Could you help me measure its wingspan?' she asked.

Ulf took one end of the measuring tape, and together they stretched it between the tips of the vampire's wings.

'Seven point nine metres,' Dr Fielding measured, and she made a note in her pad. 'Now, let's take a blood sample, Ulf.'

Ulf watched as Dr Fielding fetched a syringe from her medical box, then ran her hand over the vampire's front. She was feeling it with her fingers. 'Its chest is protected by a fused ribcage, making it difficult to penetrate.'

Ulf put his hand on the vampire's chest. He could feel that it had thick, hard ridges across it.

'It's not totally solid, though,' Dr Fielding said. 'The top two ribs aren't fused. They need to remain flexible since they connect to the wings.' She pushed her syringe between the upper two ribs and the needle plunged into soft flesh.

Ulf noticed Hurricane Stoat leaning over his shoulder. 'How interesting,' the photographer said. 'A weak spot, eh?' He clicked a photo as Dr Fielding drew out a sample of blood.

'Why are we taking its blood?' Ulf asked her.

'To test what it's been feeding on. Vampires can't produce their own blood, Ulf. This is the blood of its prey.' She put the syringe back into her medical box. 'We can only take a tiny bit. Vampires are easily weakened if they lose much blood. They're unable to replenish it without feeding.'

Dr Fielding took out two specimen jars from her box. She handed one to Ulf. 'Would you check its skin for parasites, please? Pop them in the jar if you find any.'

She knelt down to look in her medical box, and Ulf felt in the vampire's fur, inspecting it closely. He pulled out three small black worms from its shoulder. They wriggled as he dropped them into the specimen jar.

Hurricane Stoat took the jar from him. 'Urgh, how revolting,' the photographer muttered. 'Why do you want these creatures?'

'For analysis, Mr Stoat,' Dr Fielding said.

The photographer glanced down at her. Dr Fielding was scraping a sample of the vampire's poo from the ground. 'You're taking its poo, too?'

'This is an unrecorded beast, remember,' Dr Fielding replied. 'Any data we can gather will help us learn more about it.' She packed away the sample then picked up her measuring tape again. 'Ulf, can you help me measure its height. Do you think you'd be able to climb up it?'

Ulf looked up. 'No problem,' he said. He jumped up and gripped the coarse black hair on the vampire's front, then climbed up its ribs like the rungs of a ladder. At the roof of the cave, he held on to the vampire's hairy ankle and touched the end of the measuring tape to its claws. They were dug into the rock, gripping firmly.

Dr Fielding held the other end of the measuring tape to the tip of the vampire's ear. 'Height: four point two metres,' she said. 'Even bigger than I'd estimated.'

Ulf was about to climb down when he felt something round and metallic in the hair on the vampire's ankle. He looked and saw a brass metal tag attached by a thin leather strap. Engraved on the tag, he read **RSPCB-11**. 'Dr Fielding, the vampire's got a beast tag on its ankle!' he said.

Dr Fielding stared up. 'A beast tag?'

'Yes. An RSPCB beast tag.'

'Are you sure, Ulf?'

Ulf examined the metal tag more closely. 'It says RSPCB eleven.'

'Eleven? Show me, Ulf.'

Ulf parted the hair on the vampire's ankle, and Dr Fielding peered up on tiptoe, straining to see. 'Well, I never,' she said. Then she laughed and shook her head in disbelief. 'So he must have found it all along.'

'Who must?' Ulf asked. He didn't understand. 'How did a beast tag get here?'

'There's been only one other RSPCB expedition to Manchay, Ulf,' Dr Fielding replied.

'You mean Professor Farraway?'

'It seems that he must have made it here, after all.'

Ulf climbed back down and dropped to the ground. 'Are you saying that Professor Farraway *did* find the vampire?'

'It would appear so, Ulf,' Dr Fielding said. 'And he made it a code eleven.'

'What's code eleven?' Ulf asked.

'Code eleven is the highest code of protection the RSPCB can give to a beast: the denial of its existence. It would appear that the Professor chose to keep this vampire a secret.'

'I don't understand. Why would he do that?'

Hurricane Stoat stepped over. 'Perhaps it was because of those slayers,' he said. 'Maybe your Professor was trying to hide it from them.'

'Quite possibly,' Dr Fielding said.

'But why pretend it didn't exist?' Ulf asked.

'Because no one would hunt a beast that didn't exist,' Dr Fielding told him.

'But the slayers *did* hunt it,' Ulf said. 'We found them here.'

'Either way, it's nothing that matters now,' Dr Fielding said. She took her notepad out to make a note of it, then turned to Mr Stoat. 'Could you zoom in with your camera and take a photograph of its right ankle for me.'

Ulf was remembering the dead slayers, thinking back to the Professor's warning: *beware the sixth sword.* 'Dr Fielding, what happened to the Farraway sword?' he asked.

'The Professor would have destroyed it probably, Ulf,' Dr Fielding told him. 'It's not at Farraway Hall.'

'It's not?' Ulf asked. He sat down on a rock at the entrance to the cave. 'What if the Professor *didn't* destroy the sword?'

Dr Fielding was making notes in her pad. She didn't reply.

Ulf had a bad feeling that someone might have taken the Farraway sword. And he thought he knew who...

CHAPTER SEVENTEEN

Ulf glanced out of the cave. He could see Tiana and Orson exploring the crater. He ran to tell them the news about the vampire.

'Hi, Ulf,' Tiana said as he rushed over.

'Guess what?' Ulf said. 'Professor F—'

'Quiet, you two,' Orson whispered. The giant was crouched over the bones of a hammer-headed eagle. Nibbling on its wing-bone was a huge carnivorous caterpillar. 'We don't want to frighten the little fella away.'

Orson gently picked up the caterpillar, and it crawled across his hand, snuffling. 'This nibbly chap is called a morat. It's a type of scavenger beast. It feeds off the scraps that big beasts leave behind.' He placed the morat down again and it burrowed under the bones. 'It's interesting what you find in a big beast's habitat.'

Ulf was desperate to tell them the news. 'Guess what? Professor Farraway *did* find the vampire,' he blurted. 'It's got a beast tag on its ankle. A code eleven tag.'

'Well, I never. Code eleven, eh,' Orson said. 'So old Farraway was just keeping it secret.'

Tiana perched by Ulf's foot on a clump of red moss. 'A secret?' she asked.

'Mind where you're standing, Tiana,' Orson said. 'That's blood moss. You often find it where blood's been spilt.'

'Yuck!' Tiana shrieked, flying back up.

'There are all kinds of rare species down here,' Orson said. He strolled off, looking among the carcasses.

'Ulf, why would the Professor keep the vampire secret?' Tiana asked.

'I think it's got something to do with the sixth sword,' Ulf replied. 'The Professor knew something. He must have.'

147

'Like what?'

'Dr Fielding says the Farraway sword's not at Farraway Hall. What if someone else has it?'

'Who?' Tiana asked.

'Think about it, Tiana. There's one Farraway who'd really want that sword.'

Tiana frowned. 'You mean—'

'Yes,' Ulf said. 'Marackai.'

'You think *Marackai's* got the Farraway sword?'

'Why else would the Professor warn us?'

The fairy was glancing over Ulf's shoulder. 'What's Mr Stoat doing?' she asked.

Ulf looked back and saw Hurricane Stoat tugging on the climbing rope at the side of the crater. 'I've no idea,' he said.

Hurricane Stoat waved to Ulf, beckoning him over. Ulf ran to see what he wanted.

'It's time to go,' the photographer said to him.

'Already?' Ulf asked.

Hurricane Stoat pointed to the sky. 'It'll be dark in an hour or two. Dr Fielding wants us to head up now. She's just packing up.'

Ulf saw Orson striding over, carrying a writhing bundle of creepers. 'You all right, Mr Stoat?' the giant asked.

'The boy and I are just about to head back up, Mr Orson,' Hurricane Stoat told him. 'Dr Fielding asked if you wouldn't mind helping her with the rucksack.'

'Right-oh,' Orson said. 'I'll see you at the top.'

Ulf watched as Orson strode back to the vampire's cave.

Hurricane Stoat passed Ulf the rope. 'You go first,' he said. 'And quickly. We don't want to be stuck down here when that vampire wakes up.'

'Last one up's a stinky sloth,' Tiana said, whizzing off up the side of the crater.

Hurricane Stoat gave Ulf a prod. 'Well, go on then. Up you go.'

* * *

Orson peered into the cave. Dr Fielding was putting labels on her specimen jars. 'That's odd. I'm a jar short,' she muttered. She looked up, seeing the giant. 'Oh, hello Orson. Did you find anything of interest in the crater?'

'All sorts,' Orson said. 'Morats, carrion creepers, blood moss, bone beetles and corpse-hoppers.' He stepped inside and picked up the rucksack.

'What are you doing, Orson? I need that,' Dr Fielding told him.

'Mr Stoat said you wanted me to take it up.'

'Mr Stoat said what?'

'He's gone up with Ulf,' Orson replied. 'A few minutes ago.'

'Gone up? Already? But we haven't finished yet.'

'He said you told him to go.'

Dr Fielding frowned. 'I never said anything of the sort.'

CHAPTER EIGHTEEN

When Ulf reached the top of the crater, Tiana was nowhere to be seen. 'Tiana, where are you?' he called, peering into the trees.

Hurricane Stoat climbed out behind him.

'Tiana?' Ulf called again. He felt Hurricane Stoat's hand on his shoulder.

'I shouldn't worry about her,' the photographer said. 'I'd worry about yourself.'

Ulf turned to see Hurricane Stoat grinning. 'What do you mean?' Ulf asked.

'The jungle's a dangerous place,' the photographer said. 'Even for the RSPCB.' Hurricane Stoat twiddled his moustache. 'Well thank you for helping me find that vampire,'

151

he said. 'You've served your purpose now.'

Ulf could feel something crawling up his back. He saw five trembling fingers appear over his shoulder. It was Hurricane Stoat's hand. But how could it be? Hurricane Stoat was standing in front of him.

'Meet my Helping Hand,' the photographer said, grinning. 'Wriggly little beast, isn't it?'

Hurricane Stoat pulled back the sleeve of his jacket and his real hand pushed out. It had a fleshy stump where the little finger was missing!

Ulf gasped. 'You're—'

'Surprise!' Hurricane Stoat said. He threw off his hat and pulled at the skin on his neck, peeling his face back like rubber. Underneath, Ulf saw another face that was twisted like a rotten apple core.

'You're Marackai!'

'*Baron* Marackai to you,' the Baron sneered.

'You tricked us!'

'Ha ha haha ha haaah haaaaahahaaa!' the Baron laughed. He gripped hold of Ulf's arm. 'You

stupid werewolf. You fell into my little trap! Tie him up, Bone!' he called.

From behind a tree, a big man stepped out. He twisted Ulf's arms behind his back, binding his wrists together with rope. Ulf struggled, trying to free himself, but it was no use; the big man threw him to the ground and bound his ankles, then pinned Ulf down with his boot.

'You're finished, werewolf,' the Baron chuckled.

Ulf felt the Helping Hand scuttling down his collar, hiding under his T-shirt. It grasped his chest, quivering with fear. 'Dr Fielding! Orson! Up here!' Ulf called. 'Help!'

The Baron laughed as Ulf yelled. 'That's it,' he said. 'Bring them to me. I have plans for them too, just like you and your little fairy friend. Give her here, Blud.'

A small man stepped out from behind a tree, holding a butterfly net. Trapped inside it was Tiana. 'Ulf, they grabbed me,' she cried. 'There was nothing I could do.'

The Baron reached into his pocket and took

out a specimen jar. He unscrewed its lid and shook out three black wriggling worms, then he shoved Tiana inside. He screwed the lid on tightly. 'Her air will run out soon,' he said, handing the jar to Blud.

Tiana was banging her fists against the glass.

The Baron grinned, then reached into his rucksack. 'And now for my destiny,' he said. He grasped an ornate silver handle, and pulled out a long silver sword.

Ulf gasped. 'The sixth sword!' The word FARRAWAY was engraved along its blade.

'The last remaining slaying sword!' Baron Marackai said. He pointed it down at Ulf. 'Pretty, isn't it?'

Ulf gulped, feeling the sword's tip pressed to his throat.

'It's amazing the things my father left lying around at Farraway Hall,' Baron Marackai said.

'You stole it!' Ulf cried.

'It's mine by right! And now the slaying shall continue!'

'Never!' Ulf said.

Ulf felt the sword's point pressing harder.

The Baron grinned. 'You don't get it, do you? I have unfinished business with that vampire. It was *I* who sent those slayers into the jungle, years ago when I was just a boy. They had one simple instruction: follow my father and kill the beast.'

'I should have known it was you!' Ulf said, gulping.

'*I* shall not fail like they did,' the Baron sneered. 'That beast is mine! Code eleven, eh? I knew my father lied to me! I knew he'd found that vampire!'

The silver sword glinted in the evening sun as the Baron pulled it back from Ulf's throat. 'And so to business,' he said.

'You won't get away with this,' Ulf cried. He struggled as Bone's boot trod down hard on his chest. 'Orson!' he called. 'Dr Fielding! Help!'

'Sir, they're coming,' Blud said.

'Keep him quiet, Bone,' the Baron ordered.

Bone bent down and slapped his dirty hand over Ulf's mouth, then dragged him into the jungle.

Baron Marackai hid behind a tree as Dr Fielding climbed out of the crater. 'Ulf? Mr Stoat? Where are you?' she called.

The Baron tiptoed out behind her. 'I'm right here,' he said, and he bonked her on the head with the handle of the sword. She fell to the ground, unconscious. 'Splendid,' he laughed. 'And now for the giant.'

Ulf could hear the rope creaking as Orson climbed up the crater wall.

The Baron peered over the edge. 'Coo-ee!' He raised his sword and sliced through the rope.

'Aaaaaaaaaaaaaaaaaaaaaaaaaaaaaaaaaaaaaaaargh!' There was a loud thud as Orson hit the bottom of the crater.

Baron Marackai grinned. 'This is fun,' he said. 'I can't wait until that vampire wakes up to feed. I do hope it likes giant's blood.' He strode over to Ulf. 'What a shame you won't be around to watch.' Then he struck Ulf over the head with the handle of the sword, and everything went black.

CHAPTER NINETEEN

Ulf opened his eyes. It was almost dark and he was lying on the jungle floor looking up at a tree with purple berries. It was the bullberry tree where he'd hidden the night before. His head was hurting, and under his T-shirt he could feel the Helping Hand trembling. On a branch above him, he noticed a specimen jar rattling. Tiana was inside it, banging her fists against the glass. Ulf tried to get up, but his hands and feet were tied and pegged to the ground. Then he heard a *hisssssssssssssss*. Slithering down the trunk of the bullberry tree, he saw the throttle-neck serpent. Its tongue flicked out, tasting his toe.

'Dinner-time, snakey,' he heard.

Ulf glanced over and saw Blud and Bone peering over a bush, sniggering.

'Give him a cuddle, Mr Snake,' Blud said.

The huge serpent began sliding over Ulf's legs, coiling around his knees, squeezing them together. 'Get it off me!' Ulf cried.

The two men stepped from the bush. 'Goodbye, werewolf,' they said, and they headed away into the darkness.

'Enjoy the show, little fairy,' Blud called.

Ulf tried to pull his legs free from the serpent, but its coils were wrapping them tightly. He was trapped. He felt the serpent sliding up his legs, then around his back and his stomach, squeezing him. It wound around his chest, its scaly body pinning his arms to his sides. He looked up, glimpsing the pale crescent moon between the leaves. If only it was a full moon, he thought, then he'd be able to transform and break free.

Ulf tried to push with his elbows, but it was no use; the serpent was too strong. It coiled around his shoulders. The Helping Hand scuttled from Ulf's T-shirt. 'Help me,' he said to it, but the

Helping Hand quickly scurried away up the tree, disappearing among its leaves.

Ulf felt the serpent's tongue flick against his cheek. He saw its glassy eyes staring at him. Then he felt it squeeze harder. And harder. And harder. He gasped for air. Ulf was being crushed. He heard Tiana banging on the inside of the glass jar. He saw her shouting, but he couldn't make out her muffled words. Then Ulf glimpsed the Helping Hand again. It was creeping along a branch towards the jar. It gripped the lid with its fingers and quickly unscrewed it.

Tiana flew out, sparkling. 'Ulf!' she cried, flying down. She blasted sparkles in the serpent's eyes, but the serpent just hissed and coiled around Ulf's neck, squeezing even tighter.

'It's crushing me, Tiana,' Ulf gasped. In a burst of sparkles, Tiana zoomed off into the treetops. 'Come back!' Ulf called. He could feel his body going limp. He couldn't breathe.

'Try this, Ulf!'

Tiana came flying back through the trees. In her arms, she was carrying a small silver ball.

She hovered above Ulf's head. 'Open your mouth, Ulf!'

'What for—'

As Ulf opened his mouth to speak, Tiana dropped the silver ball on his tongue. 'It's a nectar sac, Ulf. From a moonflower. Bite it!'

The nectar sac felt smooth and cold. Ulf clasped it between his teeth and bit. The sac burst and moonjuice trickled over his tongue and down his throat.

Suddenly, a silver light flashed behind his eyes. Ulf felt his chest expanding and air rushing into his lungs. His hands and feet tingled as his blood heated up. Fangs grew from his gums, and his jaw lengthened. It was incredible. He could feel his body changing – he was starting to transform! His skin sprouted thick black hair and his muscles grew, snapping the ropes around his wrists and ankles, and pushing against the coils of the serpent. It was still squeezing hard, but Ulf was fighting back. He felt his bones cracking as his skeleton realigned from biped to quadruped, then his jaw thrust forwards and his face changed into that of a wolf. He snarled at the serpent. It hissed back, but he pushed his paws free, unwrapping the long scaly beast, coil after coil. He threw the serpent off him and jumped on to all fours.

'Go, Ulf!' Tiana called.

Ulf felt wild and strong. He lifted his head and howled as the serpent slithered away into the bushes. 'Thank you, Tiana,' he growled.

'It was the Helping Hand who saved us,' Tiana said.

Ulf looked up and saw the Helping Hand waving at him from the bullberry tree.

'I'll look after it,' Tiana told him. 'You save Orson and Dr Fielding.'

Ulf bounded away through the trees.

CHAPTER TWENTY

As Ulf ran he heard a spine-tingling screech. He raced to the crater's edge and looked down. His wolf senses were sharp and by the pale light of the crescent moon he could make out Orson lying unconscious on the rocks at the bottom. The vampire was circling above him, preparing to feed.

'No!' Ulf roared. He leapt from the edge of the crater, throwing himself down, his claws outstretched. He landed with a thud on the vampire's back. The beast screeched and turned its head towards him. Its eyes were blazing red.

'Leave him alone,' Ulf growled, gripping the hair on the vampire's neck.

The vampire tried to bite Ulf, but its fangs couldn't reach. With a powerful flick of its wings the vampire rolled upside down in the air, trying to throw Ulf off. He clung on tightly as the beast soared upwards, beating its wings, twisting and turning. It swerved and looped, flying out of the crater, high into the night sky. Still Ulf clung on.

All of a sudden, he heard a buzzing in the air. It was the sound of an engine. A light came on in the sky. An aircraft was shining a searchlight towards them. The vampire screeched as the light shone in its eyes. It swerved quickly to the side and Ulf gripped its wing to stop himself falling.

'There it is!' he heard. The aircraft's engine grew louder. It was flying nearer. Standing in its cockpit was Baron Marackai. He was holding the slaying sword in one hand and a megaphone in the other. 'Open fire, Bone!' he called.

As the aircraft and the vampire flew towards one another, Ulf peered over the vampire's ears. Sitting in the front of the cockpit he could see the Baron's henchmen. Blud was steering, while Bone was pointing a machine gun.

Ratatat! Ratatat! Ratatat! Bullets spat through the air towards the vampire. The vampire swerved, and the flying machine buzzed past.

'Werewolf? You're meant to be dead!' the Baron called.

Ulf hung on tightly, looking back as the flying machine turned. It was coming in for another attack. The vampire flapped its huge wings, trying to escape the Baron and his men.

'Shoot them out of the sky!' the Baron ordered. 'Both of them!'

Ratatat! Ratatat! Ratatat! The machine gun fired again and the vampire weaved left and right. The searchlight flashed on them. The vampire's wings were rippling and flexing as it rolled and dodged. It was moving so quickly that Ulf could barely hold on.

Ratatat! Ratatat! Ratatat! The vampire climbed higher and higher in the sky. It flew straight upwards and Ulf clung on with his front paws, his back legs dangling.

'Aim higher! Fill them with holes!'

Ratatat! Ratatat! Ratatat! The vampire

swooped and swerved as bullets streaked past. The flying machine was chasing them.

'Why can't you hit it? It's right in front of you!' the Baron shouted.

Ratatat! Ratatat! Ratatat! The vampire veered left then right, dodging the bullets.

'You missed, Bone, you fool!' the Baron called. 'Aim to the right! No, left a bit! Just shoot it!'

Ratatat! Ratatat! Ratatat! Bullets shot straight past on either side, but the vampire was too agile for the flying machine. It folded its wings in close, then dropped into a headlong dive, whizzing down past the Baron.

'Hold fire, Bone!' Baron Marackai ordered.

The machine gun stopped.

'Think you've won, do you, werewolf?' the Baron called. 'We'll see about that.'

Suddenly, Ulf heard a scream. He looked up and saw the flying machine above them, circling in the sky. Swinging beneath it was Dr Fielding! She was bound with a rope, dangling by her ankles. The vampire turned, smelling her scent. It flapped its wings, flying back up towards her.

'That's it, vampire. Come and get your dinner!' Baron Marackai called.

'Stop!' Ulf growled in the vampire's ear. 'It's a trap!' But the vampire soared higher, heading straight for Dr Fielding.

'Wait for it, Bone,' the Baron ordered. 'Let it come close.'

As the vampire flew towards the bait, Ulf could see Dr Fielding's face. She looked terrified. The vampire opened its jaws…

'Fire!' the Baron called.

A volley of bullets rained down, peppering the vampire's side. It screeched and stopped in mid-air. Ulf leapt up, slashing the rope around Dr Fielding's ankles. He fell back on to the vampire with her safely in his grasp. But the vampire was falling. One of its wings was hanging limply.

With one paw, Ulf held tightly to the vampire's back, and with the other he clung to Dr Fielding as the vampire spiralled down through the air screeching. They dropped back into the crater, crashing on to rocks and bones.

CHAPTER TWENTY-ONE

Ulf shook his head and staggered on to all fours. He was dazed from the fall, but still alive. Dr Fielding was lying beside him.

'Are you all right?' he growled.

She stood up shakily. 'Just about,' she replied.

Ulf looked at the vampire. It had landed in the middle of the crater. Its wings were crumpled and it was breathing heavily. Bullets had pierced the beast's skin and it had lost blood. It was still alive, but weak.

'Keep away from it, Ulf,' Dr Fielding said.

The vampire hissed, opening its fanged jaws.

'But we have to help it,' Ulf said.

'It's lost blood. It needs to feed. It will kill you.'

From overhead, a searchlight shone down into the crater. 'That beast is mine,' Ulf heard. It was Baron Marackai calling through his megaphone.

'Ulf, quick,' Dr Fielding said, pointing across the crater. 'We have to help Orson.' Ulf saw Orson lying on the rocks unconscious. Dr Fielding started running towards the giant.

Ulf glanced back at the vampire. It was struggling, flapping one wing, trying to get to its feet. It stumbled and fell. 'Don't die,' Ulf growled.

The flying machine buzzed overhead. 'Blud! Bone! Remove the werewolf!'

Ratatat! Ratatat! Bullets began firing down, hitting the ground beside Ulf.

He dived, rolling across carcasses and bones.

'Make him dance!' the Baron laughed.

'Ulf, over here,' Dr Fielding called. She was kneeling beside Orson.

Ulf leapt up and ran, a trail of bullets following him as the aircraft passed overhead. He ran in zigzags, dodging and weaving as bullets peppered the ground. Suddenly, the bullets stopped. He looked up. The aircraft was banking, preparing for another run.

'Quick, Ulf, help me get Orson into the cave,' Dr Fielding said. 'He needs medical attention.'

Ulf dug his claws into Orson's boot and with werewolf strength began dragging the giant across the ground. He heaved Orson towards the cave at the side of the crater. The flying machine's searchlight shone on them. *Ratatat! Ratatat!* Bullets ricocheted off the walls at the entrance to the cave, just as Ulf pulled the giant to safety.

Dr Fielding unfastened the rucksack from Orson's back and took out her torch and medical kit. 'He's got a nasty gash on the back of his head,' she said. The giant was out cold.

Ulf peered out from the entrance of the cave. The vampire was still struggling on the ground. The aircraft was circling overhead, its searchlight sweeping across the crater. The light shone in Ulf's eyes.

'Oh, hide-and-seek. What fun!' he heard Baron Marackai shout.

The machine gun opened fire again and Ulf ducked his head back inside. Through a hail of bullets, he saw Baron Marackai leap from the aircraft. A parachute opened above him and the Baron drifted down into the crater. He was clutching the silver sword.

The vampire! Ulf thought.

As the Baron landed, he slashed through his parachute strings. 'My destiny!' he called, marching towards the vampire, his sword held high.

Ulf was desperate to help the vampire, but the bullets were raining down, trapping him in the cave. He saw Baron Marackai kick the vampire's wing with his boot, revealing its chest. The vampire screeched, trying to lunge for the Baron, but it was too weak. Baron Marackai cackled and raised his sword, ready to strike the killer blow. All of a sudden, a volley of bullets spattered into the ground around the Baron and he glanced up. 'Bone, mind where you're shooting, you nincompoop!' Bullets were firing chaotically all around the crater.

In the sky above, the flying machine was rolling and dipping in a huge black cloud. Its

173

engine was sputtering. Ulf could see the black cloud swirling. It was a storm of encantos. They were whirling around the aircraft, attacking it.

Suddenly, the bullets stopped firing. Ulf saw the aircraft fleeing into the night, escaping the angry spirits. 'You cowards!' the Baron called.

Ulf seized his chance and ran from the cave, bounding towards the Baron. 'Leave the vampire alone,' he snarled.

Baron Marackai turned to face Ulf. 'Well, well, do I have to kill you too?' he said. The Baron stepped forward, pointing his sword at Ulf. 'HOW DARE YOU COME BETWEEN A SLAYER AND HIS DESTINY!'

The Baron swiped the sword at Ulf. Ulf dodged, but the Baron swiped again and he felt a stinging pain in his arm. The blade had cut him. 'You've messed up my plans once too often,' Baron Marackai hissed. 'Now it's time to finish you off!'

'Need some help?' Ulf heard from above. He looked up. A sparkle was zooming down towards him. It was Tiana.

'Down here,' the fairy called. Following her into the crater was the storm of encantos. Ulf felt an icy wind as they swirled down like a tornado, whirling around the Baron.

'Get off me!' the Baron cried. He was swiping at the spirits with his sword, but the blade was useless against them. He was engulfed in an icy black cloud, running in circles, screaming: 'Get off me! Get off me!'

Ulf felt the blood running from the cut on his arm. He rushed to the vampire. It was baring its fangs.

'Be careful, Ulf!' Tiana cried.

'Drink,' Ulf growled to it. He held his arm out, dripping blood into the vampire's mouth. It began to gulp. 'Werewolf blood is powerful.'

With each gulp of fresh blood, the vampire grew stronger. Slowly it rose to its feet.

'Watch out, Ulf!' Tiana cried. 'It'll bite you!'

But Ulf leant closer to the vampire. 'It's him you want,' he growled, pointing to the Baron. Baron Marackai was running from the encantos, his fur coat white with frost.

The vampire turned and its eyes flashed red. It flapped its wings and lunged for the Baron, grabbing him in its claws. It plucked him off the ground and soared into the sky, screeching.

'N-n-n-nooooooooo!' Baron Marackai cried, as the vampire carried him away into the night.

Ulf saw a flash in the sky then heard a clattering sound as the silver sword fell to the ground. Then the crater fell silent and the air cleared as the encantos dispersed.

Tiana landed on his shoulder. 'Where are Dr Fielding and Orson?' she asked.

Ulf looked across to the cave at the side of the crater. He saw Dr Fielding stepping out. 'How is he?' Ulf growled.

Dr Fielding gave a thumbs-up and Orson stepped from the cave behind her. His head was bandaged. 'Hello, Ulf,' he called. 'How come you've transformed?' Then he glanced around the crater. 'And where's Mr Stoat?'

Ulf smiled, his fangs glinting. He looked up at the moon and howled.

CHAPTER TWENTY-TWO

The next day, Ulf woke to the sound of humming engines. He was wrapped in a blanket in the cockpit of the C130 Hercules. The thick hair had gone from his face. He licked his teeth; his fangs had receded. He was no longer a wolf.

Dr Fielding was beside him. 'Good afternoon, Ulf,' she said, seeing him stirring. 'Are you feeling okay?'

Ulf could feel a dull pain in his arm. It was bandaged. 'What happened?' he asked.

'Don't you remember?'

Ulf's memory of the previous night was hazy.

'You saved our lives, Ulf,' Dr Fielding told him.

A sparkle flew from the plane's control panel.

It was Tiana. 'Ulf, you're awake!' she said. 'You went wild last night! You defeated the Baron!'

Dr Fielding smiled. 'I radioed the plane and we were picked up this morning. We're nearly home.'

Squadron Leader Steel turned to Ulf. 'Buckle up,' he said. 'Prepare for landing.'

Ulf looked out of the window of the plane. They were flying over the sea, and in the distance he could see land. Dr Fielding handed him a pair of khaki overalls from under her seat. 'Put these on,' she said. 'They're RAF issue.'

Ulf pulled on the overalls under his blanket. They were too big for him, but his T-shirt and jeans had been shredded when he'd transformed. He strapped in then watched out of the window as the plane approached the RSPCB beast park. It descended over the seawater lagoon and the Great Grazing Grounds then bumped down in the paddock. The pilot braked and the plane came to a halt.

'Welcome home,' Dr Fielding said. She opened the cockpit door. 'Thank you, T-Bone.

Come and join us for a bite to eat if you'd like.' She jumped down on to the grass and Ulf leapt out after her. It felt good to be back. Tiana whizzed past him, clasping her satchel. 'The other fairies are going to be so jealous when they see the pollen I've collected,' she said, and she zoomed off to the Dark Forest.

The cargo hold opened and Orson stepped out, stretching his arms. 'That's better.' Then he saw Ulf. 'The hero returns, eh? I hear you were brave last night.'

Ulf looked away, embarrassed. On the rooftop of Farraway Hall, Druce was waving to him. 'Hooray! Fur Face back!' the gargoyle called. He had on one of Dr Fielding's white lab coats and was jumping up and down.

Ulf smiled, following Orson and Dr Fielding back towards the yard. He saw Helping Hands filling buckets with water and dragging sacks of feed. Orson put his rucksack down. 'Thanks for looking after the place,' he said to them, tickling one with his fingertip.

From the side pocket of the rucksack,

another Helping Hand climbed out. It was the one that had saved Ulf in the jungle. 'Thanks for your help,' Ulf said to it. The hand gave a thumbs-up then scurried to join the others.

Dr Fielding took out her medical box and a blanket that was wrapped in a bundle. 'Orson, would you put the kit away, please?' she asked. 'Tell Squadron Leader Steel I'll be indoors.'

'No problem,' Orson replied.

'Ulf, would you mind giving me a hand?' she said.

Ulf carried Dr Fielding's medical box into Farraway Hall. They went to her laboratory and she placed the bundled blanket on a table then began unloading her medical samples.

'I'm extremely proud of you, Ulf,' Dr Fielding said. 'You've not only excelled in your jungle training, but you saved the vampire too.'

'Do you think it will be all right?' Ulf asked.

'It'll be fine, Ulf. You were brave to feed it like that. I've never seen that done before.'

Ulf saw the test-tube of vampire blood and remembered the jungle vampire drinking from him the night before. 'I couldn't just let Marackai kill it,' he said.

Dr Fielding reached into her pocket. 'Have a look at this, Ulf.' She took out a photograph of butterflies perched on the rock carving of the vampire. 'This was in Hurrica— I mean *Marackai's* jacket.'

Ulf looked at the photograph. It was the same as the one he'd seen in *Wildlife Weekly*, but it looked old and tatty.

'It was *Marackai* who sent this picture into *Wildlife Weekly*. He knew I'd see it. He was very clever, Ulf. He used us to find the vampire.'

'I don't understand,' Ulf said. 'When did Marackai take this picture?'

'*Marackai* didn't,' Dr Fielding said. She turned the photo over and Ulf saw handwriting on its back: Bluetail Butterflies on Drake's Ridge, by Prof. J.E. Farraway, Expedition Manchay.

'This photograph was taken by the Professor, years ago, on his expedition. Marackai must have stolen it from the file and kept it all this time, suspecting that the vampire was out there.'

Ulf remembered Marackai's words: *I knew my father lied to me…* 'It was Marackai who sent the slayers to the jungle, Dr Fielding. That's why the Professor made the vampire a code eleven – to protect it from him. He knew Marackai wanted to kill it.'

Dr Fielding shook her head. 'How wicked he is,' she said. 'He would have killed us too, if it hadn't been for you, Ulf.' She placed the photo on the table then from her medical box took out a specimen jar full of silver balls. 'It's a good thing Tiana told you about moonjuice.'

Ulf stared at the jar. It was full with the nectar sacs of moonflowers. 'When did you get those?'

'On our first night in the jungle, Ulf.'

'You mean you knew about moonjuice all along? Why didn't you tell me?'

'I didn't know if you were ready, Ulf. Professor Farraway discovered moonjuice years ago. He wrote all about its properties.' She opened a metal cabinet and fetched a large bottle of glowing silver liquid. 'He collected all this.' She pulled a cork from the top of the bottle then dropped the nectar sacs inside.

Ulf stared, amazed, as they fizzed and dissolved. 'Wow! I can go wild whenever I want.'

Dr Fielding placed the bottle back in the cabinet. 'Maybe one day, Ulf, but there's a lot to being a werewolf that you don't know yet.'

Ulf was thinking back to his transformation. He remembered flying on the vampire's back and the screech it had made as it carried Marackai away in its claws. 'Dr Fielding, is Marackai definitely gone?' he asked.

'I hope so,' she replied. 'But it's hard to say for certain. There have been times before when I thought we'd seen the last of him, and yet he still somehow returned.'

'I hope he's dead,' Ulf said.

'At least *this* is no longer a threat.' Dr Fielding unwrapped the bundled blanket. Inside it Ulf saw two silver shards of a broken sword.

'The Farraway sword,' he said.

'Would you mind taking it upstairs to the Room of Curiosities, please?'

Ulf picked up the broken sword in the

blanket, and carried it out, up the back stairs and along the Gallery of Science. There was someone he wanted to show it to. Ulf walked straight through the Room of Curiosities to the door on the far wall. It creaked open and he peered into the gloom of the old library. 'Professor, I'm back.'

On a dusty table at the side of the room a candle flickered on. Ulf stepped towards it. 'The vampire is alive and well, Professor. And we've recovered the sixth sword.'

Ulf laid the blanket on the table, and the broken silver sword glinted in the candlelight. 'Marackai can't use it now,' he said.

But as Ulf spoke, an invisible finger began writing in the dust: MARACKAI IS THE REASON YOU'RE HERE...

THE END... FOR NOW

Visit www.beastlybusiness.com
for lots of exciting extras
- meet the authors, join the
RSPCB and discover the secrets
of the beasts...!

**Turn the page for the first
two exciting chapters from**
Battle of the Zombies

BEASTLY
BUSINESS

CHAPTER ONE

It was the dead of night and high in the sky a hot-air balloon was drifting through the darkness. In its basket were three men. The tallest of them peered down through a telescope. 'We're approaching the target,' he said. 'Turn off the gas, Bone.'

'Yes, Baron Marackai,' a big man replied. He twisted a handle on the balloon's burner and its flame went out. The balloon began to slowly descend.

A small man gripped the basket, nervously sucking on a rag. 'I don't like the dark,' he said.

Baron Marackai turned, eyeing him. 'We don't want anyone seeing us, Blud, you idiot.

This is a secret mission, remember.' The Baron raised his right hand, wiggling a stump where his little finger was missing. 'Now, repeat after me: Death to the RSPCB.'

Blud and Bone quickly raised their right hands and turned down their little fingers. 'Death to the RSCPC,' they said.

'The RS*PCB*, you numbskulls.' The Baron swiped his telescope, clonking them on their noses. 'Now, silence. We're coming in to land.'

Blud and Bone peered over the side of the basket. The balloon was descending gently towards a large castle.

The balloon drifted slowly between towers and turrets then landed with a bump on the castle's rooftop.

The Baron stepped out on to the roof and looked down at the castle's outer walls where knights in armour were standing guard. 'Hah, the fools never saw us,' he muttered. 'Bone, hold the basket steady. We shall need it for our getaway. Blud, pass me the box.'

Blud and Bone climbed out. While Bone

held the basket, Blud handed the Baron a little wooden box.

Baron Marackai opened it and carefully took out two small bottles, one containing silver liquid and the other golden liquid. He grinned, watching them sparkle. 'This time the RSPCB is doomed.'

'What's the plan, Sir?' Blud whispered.

'Never you mind,' the Baron said. 'Just wait here and keep quiet.' Clutching the two bottles, he crept away across the rooftop and disappeared into the darkness.

Blud and Bone heard the rusty creak of a door opening, then the Baron's footsteps descending a flight of stone steps. They huddled together, hearing the wind whistling round the turrets and towers and strange moanings and groanings sounding from the castle's windows.

'What's he doing?' Blud asked.

Bone pointed to a walkway silhouetted between the main castle building and a tall tower. 'Look,' he whispered. The dark figure of

Baron Marackai was creeping along the walkway. There was a muffled clang then the Baron went inside the tower and a moment later reappeared with a second figure following him.

'Someone's with him,' Blud said. The two dark figures disappeared back into the main building, and Blud and Bone waited anxiously.

Suddenly, they heard shrieks and cries coming from inside the castle. Voices called out: 'It's incredible!'… 'Look at me!'… 'I'm alive!'

Then they heard footsteps running and Baron Marackai came hurrying back on to the rooftop, the second figure running alongside him. 'This way, Harold. We'll soon have you out of here,' the Baron said.

The Baron and his companion dashed to the hot-air balloon and jumped in its basket. 'Blud, Bone, get in,' the Baron ordered. 'It's time to go.'

Blud and Bone glanced at one another, puzzled, then climbed into the basket. Bone fired the burner and the balloon began to rise from the castle's roof up into the night sky.

The Baron picked a cobweb from his fur coat. 'Well, that all went rather well,' he said. 'Blud, Bone, I'd like you to meet Harold.'

Blud and Bone stared at the other man in the basket. The man had on a chainmail vest and a black leather tunic, but where his head should have been was just the stump of a neck. His head had been chopped off, and he was carrying it under his arm.

'Pleasssed to meet youuu,' the head hissed.

Blud and Bone gripped one another in terror.

'So, Harold, you're free at last,' the Baron said. 'Aren't you going to thank me for breaking you out?'

Harold held up his head to look the Baron in the eye. 'Thanksss,' it hissed.

The Baron grinned. 'That's quite all right, Harold. NOW, THERE'S SOMETHING I'D LIKE YOU TO DO FOR ME...'

BEASTLY
BUSINESS

CHAPTER TWO

It was a sunny morning at the Royal Society for the Prevention of Cruelty to Beasts, and Ulf was riding his quad bike across the Great Grazing Grounds towing a trailer full of smelly manure. He'd spent all morning in the meat-eaters' enclosure mucking out an Egyptian scorpius, a large venomous beast that was recovering from pincer-lock. Now he was on his way back across the beast park to drop the manure at the flower garden.

Ulf rode past Sunset Mountain and splashed on to the marsh where the bogwobbler was basking. He slowed his bike and from a canvas bag behind his seat he took out a bone and threw it to the beast. The bogwobbler's mouth opened like a crater in the mud, gobbling the bone whole.

Ulf sped on past Troll Crag then round the biodomes: enclosures for the extreme-weather beasts. He slowed alongside the snow dome where an ice dragon was recovering from a broken wing. Helping Hands – hand-shaped beasts that helped around the centre – were loading frozen fish into the dome's feeding cannon. They fired the fish and the ice dragon lurched, snatching the fish in its jaws. 'Good catch,' Ulf called.

As the ice dragon belched a jet of blue flames, Ulf smiled then twisted the bike's throttle with his hairy hand and accelerated away.

The RSPCB was a rescue centre for rare and endangered beasts, from washed-up sea monsters to vampires with toothache. Ulf was a beast himself, an orphaned werewolf, and had lived at the centre ever since he'd been brought in more than ten years earlier. He was now training to become an RSPCB agent.

Ulf rode into the lower paddock and saw Orson the giant wading in the freshwater lake.

'Morning, Orson,' Ulf called.

The giant glanced over. 'Morning, Ulf.'

Ulf pulled up beside the lake and saw that the giant was releasing a magnaturtle into the water. Orson handled all the large beasts. He let go of the amphibious emerald-shelled turtle and it flapped its flippers, gliding out across the lake like a floating island.

'Is it going to be all right now?' Ulf asked.

'Hopefully,' the giant replied. 'Dr Fielding operated on it. The poor thing had swallowed a plastic crate.'

Orson glanced at the manure in Ulf's trailer. He sniffed. 'Phwoar, that stuff smells 'orrible.'

'Does it? I suppose I've got used to it,' Ulf replied, smiling. He revved the bike's engine and sped away up the side of the paddock towards Farraway Hall, a large country house and the headquarters of the RSPCB.

He parked by the flower garden at the back of the house, then began unloading the manure with a shovel. Tall, thorny flowers scuttled over on their roots and wriggled into it. Ulf could hear them purring, then their petals opened red with delight. A sparkle darted up from them. It was Tiana the fairy, Ulf's best friend.

'Hey, watch out, Ulf! That stuff went on my new outfit!' she yelled, wiping her dress made from dried cornflowers.

'Sorry, Tiana,' Ulf said. 'I'm feeding the roving roses.'

The fairy sniffed. 'It stinks!'

'It's manure,' Ulf told her, throwing on another shovelful. 'It's scorpius poo – full of goodness, apparently.'

'Scorpius poo! You went in with the scorpius? You must be crazy.'

'It wasn't dangerous. I hypnotised it,' Ulf said. 'It says how to in *The Book of Beasts*.'

The Book of Beasts was Ulf's most precious possession, a notebook that had once belonged to Professor Farraway, the founder of the RSPCB, and it contained all kinds of tips and tricks on handling wild beasts.

Ulf leant on his shovel, listening to the roving roses slurp and burp as they fed.

Suddenly, he heard a loud trumpeting fanfare from the other side of Farraway Hall. 'What was that?' he said to Tiana. He looked around the side of the house and saw Dr Fielding, the RSPCB vet, rushing towards the forecourt.

'Something's going on,' Tiana said.

'Come on, let's take a look.' Ulf grabbed his bag from the quad bike and raced across the yard. He found Dr Fielding by the entrance gates, looking up the driveway. Galloping towards her was a unicorn and, riding on its back, was a knight in shining armour with a bugle in his hand.

'Woweee!' Tiana said, surprised.

Ulf watched, intrigued, as the knight pulled on the unicorn's reins and brought it to a standstill by the gates.

The knight raised the visor on his helmet and saluted to Dr Fielding. Ulf and Tiana both gasped; where the knight's face should have been was just hollow darkness. The knight's helmet was empty, as if there was no one inside the suit of armour.

'Good morning,' Dr Fielding said to the knight. 'How can I help you?'

Without replying, the knight reached down through the bars of the gate and handed her a rolled-up paper scroll. Then he closed his visor and pulled on the unicorn's reins, turning it round. With a tap of his heels, the knight rode off back up the driveway.

'Who was that, Dr Fielding?' Ulf asked.

Dr Fielding was unrolling the paper scroll. 'That was a ghost knight, Ulf,' she replied.

'A ghost!' Tiana shrieked. She perched on Ulf's shoulder, trembling.

'There's no need to be frightened, Tiana,' Dr Fielding said. 'He was just delivering a message.'

Ulf stepped beside Dr Fielding and looked at the scroll:

TROUBLE AT HOWLHAMMER CASTLE.
COME QUICK!

'Howlhammer Castle? Where's that?' Ulf asked. He'd never heard of it before.

'It's about three hours north of here,' Dr Fielding explained. 'It's an RSPCB habitat for ghosts.'

'A *haunted* castle!'

'That's right, Ulf. **It's the most haunted place in the country.** Years ago, Professor Farraway declared it a site of special cryptozoological interest and had it protected by law.'

Ulf looked back at the scroll. 'What do you think the trouble is there?' he asked.

'Hmm, a phantom with a fever perhaps,' Dr Fielding replied. 'Or a poltergeist trapped in a cupboard, or maybe a ghoul with gas? Ghouls are always getting gas. We'd better drive up there and find out.' She rolled the scroll back up. 'Would you like to come? Howlhammer Castle has all kinds of ghosts to learn about. It would be good for your training.'

'I'd love to,' Ulf replied excitedly.

'Great. All RSPCB agents should know about ghosts, Ulf.' Dr Fielding turned to the fairy. 'And what about you, Tiana?'

'I… er… I… erm…'

Ulf could feel Tiana's wings fluttering nervously against his neck. 'Don't worry, Tiana, I'll look after you,' he whispered.

'Excellent,' Dr Fielding said. 'I'll radio Orson and fetch the truck. We'll leave in fifteen minutes.'

As she unclipped her walkie-talkie from her belt, she sniffed. 'What *is* that revolting smell?'

Tiana giggled. 'It's Ulf.'

Ulf looked at his hands, still mucky with manure. 'Don't worry, Dr Fielding. I promise to have a wash before we go.'

BEASTLY
BUSINESS

**The Beastly Boys
are David Sinden,
Matthew Morgan and
Guy Macdonald. They met at
school in Kent, and have been
friends ever since.**

SIMON AND SCHUSTER
A CBS Company